Other books by Andrev

Cold Blood

To Morgan Sovine
For being an amazing beta reader and more
importantly a great friend

Cup

Of

sleep

33Andrew James King

Contents page

Andrew James King

Chapter One
Caramel Shot to the Heart

Company Policy Thirty-One: If you are caught sleeping at your desk and survive, you will be fined half a day's pay with a minimum amount being <forty-five> spunod per infraction.

The Benny Beans mascot loomed over the town like the eldritch abominations of old. City-sized eyes that watched all, heard all and knew all. They saw as the dark slender fingers of the worker in cubicle C27 typed away at her computer in the heart attack division of the Incident Report room. Elizabeth Clair's last cup of coffee was thirteen minutes and seven seconds ago yet she was already craving another.

"One minute and fifty-three seconds till Benny boost." her coffee machine explained in a monotone voice. She hit the side of the machine with shaky hands and screamed.

"I want it now! I need it NOW!" She reached for her previous cup, drank the few remaining drops and went back to work, typing slower and slower. Her screen listed, among other people,

Name: Alex Shoulder

Cup of Sleep

Gender: Invalid Response "gender-neutral they/them"
Age: 34
Address: 1 Green Meadow, Glyncorrwg", SA13 3BN
Cause of death: Power outage caused the coffee machine to shut off.
Note: Leader of Matulog

Elizabeth glanced over at the timer on top of her machine and saw she only had to wait thirty seconds for her next cup, she could already taste the refreshing liquid as it passed her lips. In her hyperactive state she looked up, her attention caught by the small red light blinking in the corner of her cubicle, she leaned closer, using the lens of the camera as a mirror to look at her brown stained teeth. In the silence of the office, all she could hear was the everpresent buzzing sound.

"No, no no!" she heard from the cubicle next to her, followed by the repetitive sound of flesh and bone slamming against metal "It can't be broken, it just can't!" Meanwhile, Elizabeth's machine produced a hot cup of coffee which she downed in a single gulp. Ignoring the burning pain and the unexpected sweetness as the timer on the machine reset.

"Can you keep it down, Alen." an impatient voice from the other side of the room yelled, "some of us are actually trying to work." The sound of his body slamming to the ground was masked by the rattling of hundreds of people typing, the names and ages of people who died of too much coffee. The loud and repetitive tapping masked the death of someone who died because they didn't drink enough coffee.

"Alen," Elizabeth complained, "did you get my order by mistake? I don't normally have caramel in mine," he didn't reply. "If you don't say anything I'm just gonna keep it, might even change my order." Yet more time passed with no reply causing Elizabeth to stand "If you're on your phone I would stop now, they can see you on camera" yet he still didn't reply "If you ignore me one more time I will take a baseball bat to your machine so help me Benny." She walked to his cubicle and looked on the ground, turning pale as she saw his face, the veins in his forehead a bright blue in contrast to his pale skin, his grey eyes wide open.

"Why hasn't Alen replied to my email?" The woman in the cubicle to the right of Alen asked, trying to see over the cubicle wall but only making her forehead visible, her short cut ginger hair unbrushed for many days. "I'm trying to confirm a shipment of printer paper but he hasn't replied." Her forehead disappeared behind the wall and reappeared a few seconds later with the rest of her face, smooth skin, green eyes, red lips and rosy red cheeks all ruined by eyes so tired that her bags had their own bags. They all wore the same thing, a deep brown one-piece outfit with a patch in the pocket that smelled of coffee.

"I don't know for sure but I think it's a code two thirty-five." Elizabeth picked up his cup and took a sip, spitting out its contents the moment they touched her tongue.

"What's a two thirty-five? Is that when the machine makes decaf instead of caffeinated?" Elizabeth reached over the wall and showed the woman what was in the cup.

"No, a two thirty-five is when it glitches and dispenses only toilet juice." She placed the cup on Alen's desk and walked around to the other cubicle, reading her name tag, Jane Ender. A woman that, at full height, was barely up to Elizabeth's shoulders with a perfectly round ivory colour face was marked by the dark rings of tiredness stacked on top of each other around her eyes.

"Then what is the code for Decaf?" She sat back at her desk and removed the codebook, scanning the index for decaf, not finding it.

"Decaf is four-five three one six." She walked to the body and grabbed its arms, dragging it to the end of the room and opened the window, the force of the wind blowing a piece of paper into her face, an advertisement for the first Sleep Plus Pod. She saw a coffee cup that made the second tallest structure in the world look like a pimple on the face of the earth, With eyes that followed her every step despite actually remaining still. The cup had a face, large brown patched lips and buck teeth exaggerated to the point of parody. "Look out below!" She kicked the corpse out of the window, watching as it hit the edge of balconies before resting on top of the pile at the bottom so tall that one could, in theory, survive jumping out of the building. The pa system suddenly shrieked to life and the voice of her boss silenced everyone.

"Can employee C27 please make their way to my office as soon as possible?" Elizabeth walked back to her desk and watched the timer beeped down when it reached zero. She snatched the styrofoam cup from her machine.

"What do you think the boss wants?" Jane asked, taking a sip of her drink

"Probably wants to ask what happened to Alen." She logged off her computer and stood up, crossing the room and walking through the series of hallways leading to his office, passing holes in the wall that despite being larger than Elizabeth herself let no air through. Not long after she arrived in the office of her boss whose door, like every other, had a poster of Benny on it. It was often joked that you could tell a person's rank in any organisation by how far down the bags under their eyes went. While this was not true, one could be excused for making this mistake if they had seen Elizabeth's boss, Harold Rincword. He was a broad-shouldered, grey-eyed bald man with a monobrow, a different colour than the hair that used to be on his head. No one knew which one was dyed and which one was his natural colour, if any of them were natural.

"What happened to Alen?" he asked, reaching into his drawer and taking out a blank incident report form and a pen. "Was it a two thirty-five?" He wrote his name and Elizabeth's at the top of the incident report.

"There isn't much to say." she explained stiffly "he went longer than fifteen minutes and died of withdrawal." He continued writing, going from page to page adding details to the report and then, on a separate sheet of paper, an address.

"I want you to go to this address and talk to his family, but don't take too long. Tell them Alen is dead, give them the bill and leave. His wife's name is Danni Davis" He printed a long and thin slip of paper like a receipt and gave it to her. "But be careful. The receipt doesn't normally make people very happy."

$$zzZ$$

"One minute!" yelled a voice from the other side of the overly bright yellow door, next to which stood a single passionflower. Three locks clicked one after another as they were unlocked and the door opened, a girl who couldn't be older than six stood, dirty skin and hair with blue eyes that appeared close to tears, yet no bags to mark tiredness. Her gaze first focused behind her, a look of recognition on her face before turning to face Elizabeth.

"Have you seen my daddy?" she asked, her voice very different from the one that spoke before. "I haven't seen him all day." Elizabeth's mouth opened to tell her but no words came out. "Do you want to talk to my mommy?" Elizabeth simply nodded and watched as the child walked further into the house and around a corner, disappearing. Five minutes later she returned, dragging her mother by the wrist, again her eyes were not marked by bags.

"Is there something I can help-" Danni looked up from the ground and at Elizabeth's face, her purple eyes meeting Elizabeth's blue, Danni's was pale, almost sickly so. She didn't finish her sentence before she collapsed to the ground, leaning against the wall.

"May I come in?" Elizabeth asked, waiting for a response before stepping through the door whose bright and repetitive colour was starting to give her a headache. Elizabeth looked at her watch and took a small cylinder out of her pocket the size of a coffee mug minus the handle. "Can I have a cup?" Elizabeth asked but, when Danni hesitated she spoke again, "I speak from experience when I say getting rid of a dead body is harder than a live one, they tend to weigh more." As if waking up from a dream, Danni shook her head, a smile spreading across her face that looked to be forced.

"Of course madam." Danni permitted as she gestured for Elizabeth to enter the living room and pointed to a chair.

As Elizabeth waited for the cup, a humming sound could be heard from beneath her. She stood up and leaned down, placing her ear against the ground trying to hear.

"What are you doing?" Danni asked, returning with the item, "Get up off the floor." Elizabeth did as she was told, taking the cup and getting the cylinder back out, pushing a button at the top. From the other end, a stream of coffee flowed that she then drank, disappointed by the lack of sweetness that came with the absence of caramel. With the caffeine in her system replenished, the machine beeped and the timer reset.

"Is this everyone?" She asked, pointing to the younger girl "I remember Alen saying he had a son." Danni's face quickly went pale.

"He's in the basement." She replied. Elizabeth stood up, making her way towards the door to the living room

Cup of Sleep

"Lead the way." With an unmistakable look of defeat on her face, Danni stood up and walked past Elizabeth, towards a door painted to look like the rest of the wall, what lay behind was a set of stairs. "I was gonna have to search the house later," Elizabeth commented, "so this is a big help." With each step, the humming sound grew louder till the bottom when they were faced with a small round room with only a single bulb to light on a lamp in the corner. In the centre of the room stood a large glass chamber, connected by a USB lead to a computer. Through the glass, which reflected her dark skin, a child could be seen, small with brown hair and eyes that could not be seen because they were closed.

"This is not what it looks like," Danni pleaded, crossing the room and opening the door to the pod lifting her son out, kissing his forehead.

"Is this a sleep plus pod?" Elizabeth asked, barely holding back vomit. "He's an unproductive!" Danni hugged him closer, covering both of his ears, one with her hand and one against her chest.

"You will not speak about my son like that!" Danni pointed to the door and told both of her children to leave.

"I'm gonna have to report you," Elizabeth explained. Without speaking, Danni raised her fist, and launched forward, jabbing Elizabeth's nose with her knuckles, causing her to stumble backwards. Her head slammed against the wall, her body crumpled and slid to the floor. Elizabeth was out cold.

$$_zZZ$$

Elizabeth was in a field, surrounded by an overwhelming silence. In this field, she was the only life in sight, not a blade of grass growing on the fire-ruined ground or a single leaf from the trees now reduced to ash. '*Fire*' she thought '*burning*', she tried not to think of the war, of the videos she was shown as a child. The whistling grew louder. "There *was always work to be done.*" Louder and louder the whistling got.

"Is there anyone out there?" She screamed. From the fog a figure emerged, a formally dressed woman with the wings of an angel growing out of her back and small white wings from the temples of her head. Without even speaking to the figure Elizabeth knew its name, Somnus. They met in the centre of the field, and embraced, then the field cleared and there was nothing but darkness.

"Find me" the words hung in her mind, spoken by Somnus.

Cup of Sleep

She heard someone knocking on the glass before she knew there was glass to knock on

"Are you okay?" Danni asked as she saw Elizabeth's eyes open, while Elizabeth had been asleep Danni had done nothing but sit in the corner panicking. It took a while for Elizabeth to realise where she was, her head was light, her throat dry and she felt the need to rub her eyes, but she couldn't because her hands were bound.

"What have you done to me?" she began shaking, rolling side to side in the cylindrical chamber, feeling as if something rolled with her, the back of the chamber was a soft pad "You made me see things!"

"No," Danni explained, "what you did is called dreaming. It's natural but we don't know why it happens." Elizabeth pushed the glass, forcing the chamber door open and collapsing to the floor before vomiting.

"Are you saying I have become an unproductive?!" she asked "we have a war to recover from and you think we have time to sleep?!" again she vomited, the mostly liquid substance stopping merely centimetres away from her feet.

"When was the last time you left the house?" Danni asked.

"I had to leave to get here," Elizabeth replied. Danni grabbed Elizabeth by the shoulder and held her up, looking into her eyes

Cup of Sleep

"The war is over. We rebuilt decades ago." she could feel Danni's grip on her shoulder tighten. Dragging Elizabeth to the door and pushing her out, slamming the door behind her. Elizabeth just sat at the door crying. She had to find Somnus. If she was real. The buzzing around her was no longer audible, instead she could hear a voice, a voice speaking of a ruined world, but she saw for the first time in her life her world was not in ruin.

Chapter Two
Fatal frappuccino

Company Policy Three-Hundred and Eighty-Two: any mention of the hot beverage previously referred to as "tea" will result in immediate and irreversible termination.

Elizabeth stood in the street, she had been running for an hour and now was staring at the poster for exactly five minutes. When she heard the beeping, a repetitive and high-pitched sound that made everyone around her stop and look. She waited, hand on her heart for what she knew was gonna happen, yet another ten minutes passed and there she stood, hand still on her heart which beat at the same rate as before, staring at the poster. A woman in formal wear with wings sprouting from her back, in one she carried a sign with the number four-hundred and eighty on and in the other was a pill, lavender in colour imprinted with a shut eye. In bold, at the top of the poster were seven words taught to them from a very, very young age.

"*A productive citizen has already beaten Somnus.*"

1717Andrew James King

It's been their motto since the end of the war, '*Always be productive.*' She leaned against the wall and slid down accidentally ripping off some Benny posters, reaching into her pocket and finding a mirror, and for the first time she could remember bags did not mark her eyes, she didn't need to fight to keep her eyes open and the world seemed still, no longer spinning on its axis.

"Where have you been?" An unseen voice asked, taking a seat next to Elizabeth. "You've been missing for eight hours. If I didn't know any better, I would say you were asleep, but you would **never** do that." Jane placed her arm around Elizabeth's shoulder and rested it. "Wanna talk about it?"

"Shouldn't you be at work?" Elizabeth asked, taking Jane's arm and removing it.

"This is work" she explained "You were missing for a long time. Harold was worried and told me to try and find you. I bet people are already saying you're dead." Jane stood up and faced the wall, ripping the poster off the wall.

"Do you know who Somnus is?" Jane asked, folding it up and placing it in her pocket.

"The devil," Elizabeth answered, raising her hands and using her fingers to imitate horns.

"Not quite." She explained "Somnus is the goddess of the unproductives. Of course, they weren't called unproductives when she was worshipped but that was before the war." Jane held her hand out and grabbed Elizabeth's, pulling her up with all her strength. "How did you survive anyway," She asked, "You only had enough coffee for six hours and it has been over eight." She leaned closer and, with two fingers, touched the area beneath Elizabeth's eye. There was a look of fear on Jane's face unlike any Elizabeth had seen before but it didn't last long, quickly replaced by anger.

"I know what this looks like." Elizabeth begged, "but I can explain." Jane stumbled back and raised an accusatory finger.

"You have become an unproductive." She looked at her watch and accused.

"You have till I drink my next coffee to explain what happened and why it's not what it looks like." Once Jane finished speaking, Elizabeth began.

"Alen is dead. And I was told to tell his wife. I arrived at her house when she opened the door-" Elizabeth suddenly thought about Danni's children, if she remembered correctly names were Charlie and Sarah. "Before I continue, what happens to the children of unproductives?" she asked "are they taken to a new home?" with no change in her blank expression Jane replied

"They are killed." she affirmed, her face still unchanging "we cannot let their corrupted minds age. Why? Did she have children?" Elizabeth looked around and for the first time she truly saw the buildings she visited and passed every day, they stood tall and whole, only two of them in disrepair and those were a demonstration of the war.

"No," she continued, "never mind, let's just say I was kidnapped. Because I actually was, so we don't need to pretend." She felt the sudden and irresistible desire to touch her face and look away from Jane. Without speaking, Jane took out her phone and turned around,

"I've found an unproductive," she reported before going silent and lightly nodding to herself. "yes," again there was silence "no," yet more silence "she's fine. Someone forced her to become an unproductive." She put her phone away and turned back around "it's okay," she comforted. "The voluntary unproductives have been dealt with." Jane hugged her, placing one hand on the back of her head and the other on her shoulder.

"But she has children." Elizabeth objected as Jane's hand began moving up and down, rubbing in a repetitive and comforting pattern.

2020Andrew James King

Cup of Sleep

"I know," she replied, "it's tragic but necessary. We don't want them to grow up even more unproductive. We're recovering from the war, we don't have time to be unproductive." she began whispering in Elizabeth's ear though no words could be heard.

"Later today they will be eliminated. Probably starting with the children and ending with any adults." They separated, Jane keeping her hands on Elizabeth's shoulders. "But there's a plus side to this."

"How?" she questioned, louder than she intended, "two children are going to die."

"But," Jane countered, "this means Alen was able to resist becoming an unproductive. We can beat them." A smile of pride spread across her face. She reached into her pocket and held out a plastic bag, the bitter smell of coffee clung to it.

"Chocolate-coated coffee bean?" she asked, taking one of the sweet beans out of the bag and eating it.

"I can't believe you!" Elizabeth felt sick,

"What?" Jane replied "For when you want the taste of coffee but you don't want anything hot.

"Two children are about to die and all you can focus on is sweets." With one hand Elizabeth knocked the sweets out of Jane's hand, watching as they scattered on the floor, her nose became overwhelmed by the smell.

"To be fair they're the children of an unproductive so the world won't miss them too much," she replied, reaching into the bottom of the bag hoping to find one that survived the fall.

"I shouldn't have to tell you about the unproductives. How uncivilised they are." As she laughed she leaned down and picked up a handful of the fallen sweets and with her other hand used her mini machine to produce another cup of coffee, mixing the sweets into it, some of the water from puddles on the ground mixing with the spilt coffee.

$$zZZ$$

When Elizabeth arrived at Danni's house the raid was already in progress. At least five cars were parked outside, behind each car stood two police officers, bulletproof barista-themed aprons wrapped tightly around their waists. One of them had a megaphone.

"We know you're in there." The police officer in the middle yelled "come out with your hands up and your sleep pod available for dismantling and your death will be relatively painless." They each had drawn their guns when he continued "if you do not come out we will be forced to come in and at that point, we cannot be held accountable for what we do." a crowd began to form as the door opened, slowly the five-year-old Sarah walked out, holding a cup so big one hand was not enough.

"My mommy is trying to-" before she could finish speaking, the bullet pierced her skull, the fragment of metal shattering bone and brain before coming to an abrupt halt in the wall on the other side of her. A thunderous applause erupted from the crowd with screams of unproductive and how she deserved it. Yet Elizabeth just stood there, watching as a single drop of blood rolled down the wall and onto the floor. She did not attempt to get closer until the police did, she followed them into the house and down the stairs into the basement. Where the pod stood earlier was now empty, the only proof of its existence being a patch on the ground a lighter shade than the rest due to a lack of dust. Danni approached Elizabeth, grabbed her by the collar and pushed, forcing Elizabeth against the wall.

"This is all your fault." She looked like she was going to do more, but with three guns to the back of her head all she could do was kneel down, hands above her head, eyes closed tightly. Yet she was not shot, instead, a new officer grabbed her by the arms and pulled, forcing her to her feet.

"What will happen to her?" Elizabeth asked the guard who was leading her out of the room.

"You must be Elizabeth," he was sorrowful

"Yes, I am," she answered

"It's a shame what they did to you, just thinking of how much work you lost sickens me. Don't worry. An example will be made of her."

"What happened to my daughter?!" Danni yelled "What have you done to Sarah?!" but she did not need to wait for an answer. She collapsed to the ground, the only thing stopping her from landing on the stony ground being the police who grabbed her arms. She was led out of the house, face stained with tears and forced into a car, Elizabeth followed in a taxi.

zZZ

When both cars stopped it was in front of a cafe. Elizabeth waited, watching as, by herself, Danni left the car and walked into the cafe, showing no sign of being forced or restrained. Elizabeth paid for the taxi and left, approaching the door and pushing it open. She was immediately greeted by hot, coffee-scented air and an over-eager member of staff.

"How may I help you madam?" he asked, a smile that revealed all of his coffee-stained teeth.

Cup of Sleep

"I'm meeting a friend here," she explained, attempting to look over his shoulder, and ultimately failing.

"Shouldn't you be at work?" he asked

"Unfortunately there was a code two twenty-six," he didn't reply, just letting her pass. Danni was at a table at the very centre of the room.

"Is this seat taken?" Elizabeth asked as she approached and leaned against it.

"You shouldn't be here," Danni whispered. A drink rested in the middle of the table, a frappuccino. She did not look angry, just upset, the tears had stopped but her eyes were still marked with red. Elizabeth looked at the menu and saw the price of added Cinnamon powder, <three> spunod per drink.

"That makes two of us" Elizabeth countered, taking a seat opposite Danni. "I'm sorry about Sarah," she filled the silence. "I didn't know they would kill her."

"I don't blame you." That was all she explained before taking a long sip of her drink.

"You seemed angry at me when we met back at your house. You shoved me against the wall." Then she saw it, something small and metal floating to the surface of the drink.

"I wanted them to think I hate you." she explained, "it would make talking to you without looking suspicious easier."

"They're lying to us? Arent they?" Elizabeth asked.

"What do you mean?" Danni replied.

"All my life I've been told that we haven't recovered from the war, that the fact that we are not allowed to sleep is for our own good but that's wrong."

"Yes," Danni answered "that's why we exist, why Matulog exists, so we can make people see what they are doing. And we need as much help as we can get."

"Why are you telling me this?" Elizabeth asked

"Because I know, unlike most people here, you can be saved." Yet Elizabeth was focused not on what Danni had just said but instead on the small metal sphere which was now beeping.

"Is that-" Elizabeth began asking, but was cut off.

"A bomb? Yes, yes it is." she whispered "but don't worry, I have a plan." she winked.

"How do you expect me not to worry there is a bomb in your coffee." Elizabeth whispered with a strained voice. "Where did you even get it from?"

"They gave it to me. Trying to frame me," Danni shushed "You have to trust me, I have a plan."

Cup of Sleep

"Could you please explain the plan to me?" Elizabeth asked, she picked up the cup and looked inside, the explosive was about the size of the tip of her thumb

"The bomb will go off," she explained "when the drink is empty. How fast can you run?" Not giving Elizabeth any time to reply, with one fluid motion she took the drink from her and stood up "There's a bomb in this drink, everyone out!" she yelled, throwing the drink across the room. Yet no one reacted. Danni grabbed Elizabeth's arm, running towards the door as the liquid poured out of a hole in the side of the plastic cup. They only stopped running when they were on the other side of the road in an alleyway in between two houses whose walls were lined with posters talking about the demon Somnus, bracing themselves for the force of the blast. Nothing happened.

"Are you sure it was a bomb?" Elizabeth asked, lowering her arms. "it could have been something less sinister?"

"Yes, I'm sure it was a bomb. Just taking a while to go off." So they waited, watching the people in the cafe go about their business like there was nothing.

"Can't you help them?" Elizabeth asked.

"I could, in theory, but they would just report us. Which would be bad news for everyone involved. I did what I could to warn-"

Andrew James King

Boom!

2828Andrew James King

Chapter Three
To Sleep Beneath the cinnamon

Company Policy Nine: The standard-issue PCD (Portable Coffee Dispenser) can hold a maximum of nine hours of coffee but the standard-issue load will only include six hours or twenty-four cups.

Other than the ringing, which seemed all-encompassing, what Elizabeth noticed more was the dust. Small particles danced around her head and face before landing in her eyes, blinding her. Still, her ears rang, and still, the dust flew coming to a halt at her feet.

"Are-okay-?" Danni asked half of her words cut off by the ringing and the screams.

"Yeah, I'm fine," Elizabeth replied. Danni reached down, placing her dry, dust-covered hand over Elizabeth's mouth.

"why-you-loud?" she stuttered, pulling her hand away and extending one finger to Elizabeth's lips. Without speaking Elizabeth nodded, yet she thought '*why does she think I'm yelling. I'm not yelling.*' Half walking half running Danni led Elizabeth through the bits of rubble on the ground and round a corner into a nearby alleyway, the police responded quickly, surrounding the building and pointing weapons at any gaps a person could walk out of.

"Do they think you're dead?" Elizabeth asked, leaning against the wall.

"Sorry to say but they think we're both dead. I wouldn't recommend going home." Without speaking Elizabeth reached into her pockets and took out her coffee dispenser, empty. Danni reached into her pocket and gave Elizabeth a small reflective packet, the label was unreadable.

"What's this?" Elizabeth asked, ripping open the packet, dipping her finger and placing the bitter powder in her mouth.

"Coffee." she assured, "You've had it for pretty much every day of your life." Elizabeth looked at the packet again, trying to see the logo.

"But there's no funny coffee cup on the front." She flipped the packet over and looked on the back, its label listing every ingredient in Benny's except one, Byritherol.

"That's because it's not Benny Bean. This is the last packet you'll be getting, from now on you will be sleeping, like me." Danni stood and walked off without waiting for Elizabeth to catch up.

"But how?" Elizabeth questioned "the sleep pod was gone. Remember? I was in the basement when the police raided your house." Danni remained silent as she ran from the alleyway, across the street and to an almost identical alleyway on the other side, she turned and gestured for Elizabeth to follow saying "You have to trust me, I know what I'm doing."

" Where are we going?" Elizabeth asked, following her at a significantly slower pace. Instead of speaking she just pointed up. Elizabeth followed her finger and found she was pointing at a factory, a large perfectly shaped cube building with over twenty-five chimneys that dispensed a dirty brown, yet somewhat pleasant smelling gas. On the side of the building in big sharp letters the words "Benny Beans Cinnamon" '*Cinnamon,* Elizabeth thought breathing in the fumes, *more expensive than gold by weight.*'

"Welcome to the hiding place of the last remaining Sleep Plus Pod," Danni greeted, again she left the alleyway and approached the building, stopping just outside the fence and turning right. They walked around the perimeter of the building, stopping at every corner for Danni to look around for anyone else until finally, they found a narrow hole in the ground barely big enough for one of them at a time, the head of a ladder stuck out. Danni went first, sitting at the hole with her legs over the edge, waiting, breathing deeply before grabbing the ladder and climbing down into the darkness. Elizabeth followed feeling the rough rock scraping against her back as she descended the ladder towards a familiar humming noise.

zZZ

"Be careful up there." Danni yelled from below "some of the rungs are older than the rest and have started to rust." As she finished her words, Elizabeth reached a new rung which came loose, causing her to fall downwards. The momentum caused her to scrape her arm against the wall, enough to draw blood before she caught herself on a lower rung. "Are you okay?" Danni asked, slightly panicked, "We're nearly at the bottom so I'll be able to take a look at it there." Elizabeth continued climbing, past rats and fungus that ran down the bottom half of the pit. Elizabeth climbed till her feet touched solid ground. Danni walked over and moved Elizabeth's sleeve to the side, feeling along the cut from shoulder to her elbow. She reached into a box next to the ladder and took out bandages which she wrapped around Elizabeth's arm.

"Why haven't you done anything to replace the ladder?" Elizabeth huffed.

"You would not believe the amount of police officers that have tried to climb down and fallen to their deaths." Danni explained, "it's the best security system this place has." Through the door on the opposite side of the room stood a bigger room, one made of concrete with pipes of more colours than could be counted on one hand, sticking out of the walls plain in design but one labelled input and the other output, the basement of the factory.

"Aren't you worried about employees finding us?" Elizabeth asked, trying to count how many pipes came through the room Danni had chosen.

"No," Danni said "At first I was but then I learned this room was off-limits to the staff, too many people sampling the product. The managers can come in but they rarely do because of the murder." She said nothing to elaborate and Elizabeth didn't want to know more so she kept quiet, Looking around the poorly lit room for the sleep pod, guided in the search by the humming noise the machine made when it was being used.

"Is there someone else in here?" Elizabeth asked, feeling along the wall for a light switch.

"Please no questions," she said, "If by the end of this day you still have questions I will answer them for you but for now I'm trying to let my son sleep." She walked into the darkness and stood there for a moment, a series of beeps could be heard as she pressed buttons Elizabeth could not see. "We can let him out now," Danni said, followed by another beep and the whole room being illuminated by lights hanging haphazardly from the ceiling and walls. . His eyes shot open a look similar to when she first saw Sarah but it was accompanied by a smile.

Elizabeth just stood there, watching as Danni carried Charlie to a nearby table and sat him down, placing some cereal in front of him. He just sat there, fingers wrapped loosely around the plastic spoon in the bowl.

"Where's Sarah?" He asked, "Shouldn't we wait for her before we start eating?" He just sat there, watching as the cereal became soggy.

"Sit down." Danni told Elizabeth "You must be hungry." Elizabeth found the nearest chair and sat down, facing Charlie who remained unblinking. A plate of buttered toast and a cup containing a pale brown liquid was placed in front of her, steam still rising from the bitter-smelling drink. Elizabeth grabbed the handle and lifted the drink, her eyes widening as it burned her tongue.

"What is this discount coffee??" She demanded in disgust as white paper packets were thrown in a pile on the table in front of her. "Is that sugar?" she raised an eyebrow, ripping the packet open and dipping her finger in and licking it.

"It's called tea," Danni explained, adding three of the sweet packets into a cup of her own, mixing it with a small metal spoon. "I'm sorry I forced you into this." She said between sips of her tea. "But you do understand why I had to put you in the sleep pod. I wouldn't have done it if I had any other choice." Danni reached over and took a slice of toast from Elizabeth's plate.

Cup of Sleep

"I understand." Elizabeth acknowledged, "if you just left me unconscious on the ground I would have died, the pod saved my life." She looked over at the pod and for the first time truly saw what it looked like, a two-metre tall cylinder with a glass front and a white back, out of which wires and pipes looped, for electricity and oxygen. "We were never allowed to learn about them but during my first day of work I found one in a secret compartment behind my Boss' wall," Elizabeth explained, taking a slice of toast and using her spoon to better spread the butter. This made Danni stop eating and look forward, asking,

"Was Harold Rincword an unproductive?"

"No," Elizabeth explained "This was the person before Harold, the one Harold killed to get the job." For the next hour no one spoke, Elizabeth and Danni did work of maintaining the sleep pod while Charlie just sat there, tapping his feet and looking around the room silently, "He has barely said a word since what happened with Sarah, he just asks where she is." Danni explained, "Even though he saw the whole thing through the security camera in the plant pot."

"Do you want me to talk to him?" Elizabeth asked, "He might need someone who doesn't remind him so much of her." Without speaking she nodded, placing her tools down and sitting on the floor. "I don't mean to intrude," Elizabeth continued "But I think you might need someone to talk to as well."

"I just need to be strong." Danni retorted softly, "I need to be strong for Charlie." Elizabeth left Danni on the floor and approached the table, taking the seat she sat on before.

"Hey, buddy." She said, pushing the bowl of soggy cereal to the side "Aren't you hungry?" she asked.

"I'm waiting for Sarah," he explained, "mom says we can't eat until the whole family is at the table." he took a sip of his orange juice.

"Can I tell you something your mom doesn't want me to tell you?" Elizabeth asked. He nodded though his facial expression did not change, he just sat there, tapping his foot. "Where's the cereal?" Elizabeth asked, looking around the room, her eyes slightly now adjusted to the lack of light. Charlie pointed to a table on the other side of the room on which lay a plastic plain bowl, a box of nondescript cereal and a mini-fridge in which Elizabeth assumed she would find milk. She stood up, approached the table and opened the fridge where she did find the milk, but also something else. In a plastic bag, the top sealed by tape was what looked like a gun, but where the clip should have gone was a series of exposed wires looping into the gun and over the top into the barrel. Elizabeth put that to the side for the moment and made cereal, adding first the milk, then cereal, and finally a coffee spoon full of sugar over it.

"Thank you," Charlie said, taking the spoon out of his old bowl and placing it in the new one. "Where's Sarah?" he asked, still refusing to eat.

"She had food earlier," Elizabeth told him

"Why did she have food without me and mom?" He asked, dropping his spoon with one hand and passing it to another.

"She's with your dad," Elizabeth answered, immediately regretting it afterwards

"But dad had gone to work." He replied, "Why would she be with him?"

"She wanted to know what your dad does for a living." She answered, lacing her fingers together to hide her now shaking hands.

"What if I wanted to find out?" He asked, "I might want to work the same job as dad." Elizabeth replied, the most honest she had been since the conversation began.

"Trust me, you don't." She said, pushing the bowl closer to him."What is your least favourite part of school? Mine was being forced to sing the national anthem." He picked up his spoon and began eating, only pausing to ask,

"The what?" Before going back to eating. Elizabeth placed her hand against her chest, forming like

one would hold the handle of a mug of coffee, breathed in
and sung

> "We prepare our brew
> For the very tired few
> Sugar packs we pour
> Never more than four
> For Benny do we live
> For Benny, do we Drink."

He said nothing, simply sitting there and eating his cereal,
looking up at Elizabeth with wide eyes, hands shaking.

"My mom said we shouldn't talk about Benny. She
told me he was evil." From the sleep pod, Danni spoke up,

"If you are talking about Benny please stop,"
Danni said, speaking loudly but not aggressively, "I do not
allow such talk at the table." She stood up off the floor and
approached the table, pulling out a chair next to Elizabeth
and sitting down. "Come to the roof later, I want to show
you something."

Chapter Four
The Misspelled Name

Company Policy Three-Hundred Eighty: All production buildings with a rank higher than three must be equipped with a breath lock for the monitoring of coffee intake.

Gun in hand, making no attempt to sneak, Danni walked down the metal walkway, Elizabeth following behind her keeping her head down. While gas mask wearing employees walked over the walkway on the opposite side of the room, separated by large vats, containing what smelled and looked like powdered cinnamon. Danni had one of those uniforms but Elizabeth was still wearing the clothes she was before, though more ripped and ash-covered than before.

"Step one," Danni said, "We need to get you a uniform, not only will the mask hide your face but it will also protect you from the fumes deeper in the factory." They kept walking, cutting through factory floors, watching as people took coffee spoons full of power and poured it into small silver pouches. They were decorated with the logo of the Benny Beans Corporation Cinnamon Branch, which looked exactly the same as the regular mascot but a shade of brown everyone called Cydneymon.

Elizabeth reached around one of the workers, picked up one of these pouches and placed it in her pocket, she reached again, but this time her wrist was grabbed by the worker who looked at her and said

"If you want cinnamon powder you must pay, like everyone else." He spoke with a strong yet unplaceable accent.

"No way, do you even know how much that costs?" She struggled, trying and failing, to push past him to grab one of the packets. Danni joined him in grabbing her wrist, but pulled back, freeing Elizabeth's arm from the employee's grasp.

"Sorry about Claire," Danni addressed the employee, "It's her first day." The employee mumbled to themselves, before turning back around and resuming work.

"Who's Claire?" Elizabeth whispered as Danni dragged her away from the employee.

"You're Claire." Danni replied, "Now try to avoid drawing attention to yourself." Their footsteps got quicker, louder as they walked through the workers keeping their heads down ending at a door, to the right of which was a machine that looked like a horn. Danni produced from her pocket a device, a small, silver cylinder with a button on top, she held the device above her head, tilting it into her mouth and pressing the button, a deep brown liquid poured from the device into her mouth, her eyes widened and pupils dilated. "Your turn." She said, giving Elizabeth the device, her expression quickly changed to one of disgust "Never liked the stuff." She commented as Elizabeth took the device and did the same thing. '*Coffee*' Elizabeth thought '*Is that actually what it tastes like?*'

"Is this coffee?" Elizabeth asked, holding the device as far away from herself as possible, the bitter smell, she didn't notice before sticking to her nose. Ignoring her, Danni simply instructed her to follow. Immediately Elizabeth felt the effects, her hands shook, head ached and something else, a voice in her head whispered to her,

"You need more," It said, "You will die if you don't have more." She closed her eyes, breathing in and out.

"Breath into that." Danni told her, pointing at the machine. "It will detect the coffee on your breath and unlock, I'll be a few seconds behind." So she did, blowing into the lock and waiting for a metallic snap to mark the sudden shifting of pins. The door opened loudly, yet none of the employees shifted, continuing their work as if nothing had happened. Elizabeth walked slowly into a blue-tiled room and stood facing two doors, one on the left labelled female and one on the right labelled male. In the centre, about the same size as the other doors was a poster, in the large text it read

Fear

The

other

Elizabeth pushed open the female door and entered, running her hand along the lockers that covered the walls, the room was empty.

"Over here." She hadn't seen Danni enter the room but she was standing at the opposite side, next to an open locker, Cydneymon in the back of the locker drawn with glow in the dark paint, Danni held the uniform in one hand and a gas mask in the other, on the light blue denim dungarees was a name tag that read Claire Black. "I'll wait outside," Danni said, "get dressed and meet me there, we're heading to the roof." Without shutting the locker, under the gaze of Cydneymon, she got dressed removing the ripped and muddy shirt and jeans, replacing them with dungarees that were too big in some places, mostly arms and legs and too small in others, mostly waist and shoulders. She left the changing room, carrying the gas mask under her arm. Stopping at the door to tuck the bottom of the uniform into itself so she wouldn't trip and to put her mask on.

"Why are we going to the roof?" Elizabeth asked, approaching the door and pushing it open.

"This," Danni answered, holding her gun "Is a one-way communicator. Point it in the sky and shoot, if my maths is correct it will bounce off an orbital receiver and hopefully, the resistance Matulog, will receive the message and know I have the last pod." Danni followed Elizabeth through the door, stopping only a step past and gesturing for Elizabeth to do the same. "From now on," She explained, "My name is Alice Cross and your name is Claire Black and I'm your welcome buddy." She took a Portable Coffee Dispenser and gave it to Elizabeth "Drink *only* when I tell you to." Elizabeth followed Danni through the room, stopping occasionally as Danni felt the need to introduce her to the other employees. Joseph, Milliard, Sarah and Hannah on the left and Neil, Jack, Martha and Annabeth on the right.

"Is Alice giving you a tour of the place?" one of them asked, "hope you enjoy your first day," she looked down at the name on her tag, "Claire," she finished.

"My name's…" Elizabeth started, catching herself mid-sentence "my name is Claire." She walked away quickly.

The path to the roof was a spiral staircase found in the centre of the factory that was barely wide enough for one person at a time so Elizabeth let Danni go first, watching as she ascended the stairs, cautious as the steps creaked under her feet. Elizabeth followed, walking up slowly, yet they still creaked.

"Take a drink," Danni commanded, removing the device from her pocket and removing her mask. Elizabeth did the same, pouring the bitter-tasting liquid she had once developed a liking for, into her mouth without milk, sugar or other such additives that change the flavour.

"I need more coffee." She struggled, her hands shaking more violently, "Let go of me!" Danni's hand covered her mouth, fingers close to blocking her nose.

"When we get back I am putting you in the pod." Danni snapped, "Now give me the PCD." She held her hand out, taking the posture of a mother who wasn't mad but disappointed in their child. Yet Elizabeth still resisted. She pulled her arm back, slamming her elbow on the thin metal wall of the stairway, a numb feeling radiating up her arm and loosening her grip on the PCD.

"I need it!" Elizabeth cried, "I'll die without it!" She lashed out, but in her haste, she dropped the device which rolled to a stop at the bottom of the step in front of Danni. Before Elizabeth could react, picked it up and shoved it in her deepest pocket,

"Now keep quiet," She demanded. "If we keep quiet we can make it to the top without being interrupted." Elizabeth stood there, foot-tapping out of control and focused not on the sudden boost of energy but instead on the taste, the bitter dirt-like taste that hung in her nostril and made her eyes water. With clenched fists and sweat dripping from her forehead, Elizabeth continued walking, always one step behind Danni, resisting the urge to reach out and take her PCD back. With each deep breath she felt it pass, yet the feeling never truly did. Her hands shaking progressing to what felt like a headache as she ascended the stairs.

$$zZ$$

It was colder than both Elizabeth and Danni remembered, their breath visible as they reached the roof and pushed open the near-frozen shut door and stood atop the stone littered roof surrounded by chimneys spewing the brown powder into the air. Danni took a watch out of her pocket and looked at the time, aiming her gun into the air. At first, the sound was low and deep, Elizabeth felt her body shake with the waves, the pitch increased, before silence. There was a word on the side of the gun now, flashing in neon light, it read "mutooloog".

"What does that mean?" Elizabeth asked, pointing at the side of the gun at the word which was now glowed duller.

"It's the name of the resistance movement." Danni answered

"You spelled it wrong," she said, searching her pockets for any paper, unable to stop laughing.

"No," Danni countered, "I spelled it right, m u t o o l o o g." Danni explained

"I have a feeling you used to be a barista," Elizabeth stated, stopping at the door.

"I fail to see how that's relevant," Danni said, checking the spelling on the side of the gun.

"M a t u l o g." Elizabeth corrected leaving a significant pause between each letter spoken, it's the Tagalog word for Sleep.`` She lowered her arms, her grip on the gun loosening to the point where she almost dropped it, but at the last second caught it and sighed to herself saying, "spelling was never my strong point." before placing the gun on the ground and sitting, flinching as she sat on sharp stones.

"Do you think they got it?" She asked, watching the door,

"I don't know," Elizabeth replied, "They might have but I don't know how that thing works." She stepped away from the door and approached Danni, clearing the floor of stones with her feet before sitting down.

"I didn't invent this, you know." Danni said "It was…" she paused, a lump developing in her throat, "Alen." For the first time since they had met, she broke, her head tucked between her legs. Tears streaming down her red marked face wiped away by shaking hands. "I'm sorry." She said, attempting to stop "I didn't want to… in front of Charlie." Silently Elizabeth put one shaking hand on Danni's slender arm, her mouth uncomfortably dry. Without speaking they sat, Danni cried and Elizabeth held her, ending with the sound of footsteps echoing on the stairs and the creaking of the weak metal. "Put your mask on," Danni instructed in a barely audible whisper, Elizabeth obeyed, placing the uncomfortable silicone mask on her face.

"Hello." The voice from the doorway yelled. The colour drained from Elizabeth's face.

"It's Jane," Elizabeth whispered, watching her co-worker pass through the door and slowly approach

"Who?" Danni asked, looking up at the approaching woman.

"The person who reported you as an Unproductive." Elizabeth saw Danni's fist clench, yet her facial expression was hidden behind a mask through which only her eyes were barely visible, even her voice was distorted by the filter.

"I'm looking for someone." Jane said as she approached the pair "She's about this tall," she said, using her hand to show Elizabeth's height "Blue eyes, black hair, dark skin and a bit of an American accent." Elizabeth looked down, doing what she could to avoid eye contact.

"No madam." She said, hoping the mask distorted her voice enough. Jane's pointed look drifted, swapping from Elizabeth to Danni

"What about you?" She asked "earth to Alice," She said, reading the hunched over woman's name tag,

"Have you seen Elizabeth?" Danni replied, the sound of her teeth grating audible through the mask

"I have not," She said, attempting to regain her appearance of professionalism.

"A worker saw someone matching her description attempting to steal some cinnamon from the production line." She explained, "I was sent to collect her, Harold thought she was dead but when the report was sent out, I was sent." She turned her back, causing Elizabeth to breathe a sigh of relief, but in no way lessening Danni's anger. "Did you hear what I did earlier?" She asked, still facing away from them.

"What did you do?" Danni asked under her breath,

"I caught two unproductives today," Jane replied. Before Danni could do anything Elizabeth grabbed her arm, pulling her away from the unaware Jane who continued speaking, "And one of them was shot right in the head like. Bang!" she said, using her hands to mimic the gun that shot Sarah. Once they were on the stairs Danni took her mask off, her shortly cut ginger hair ruffled by the strap.

"I'm gonna kill her," Danni said, her jaw clenched and hands shaking.

Chapter Five
The Bitter Taste

Company Policy Four-Hundred: Any company with an employee count greater than five hundred will be provided with the opportunity to buy two litres of pure Byritherol to do with what they wish. Byritherol is the chemical that makes our coffee so powerful.

Along the back of the room a table was set, lined with a red, coffee-stained table cloth that hung over ten plastic folding chairs, a single chant echoed around the room

"Happy hour!" They yelled, both fists slamming against the conveyor belt, the packets and loose grains of cinnamon slid across without interruption. "Happy hour!" The chanting continued, increasing in pitch and volume, stopping only when a coffee cup was placed on the table in front, lacking the steam of one full of hot liquid, instead it was filled to the brim with finger-sized slips of paper folded in half, they all watched, still as a statue. Even Elizabeth and Danni paused, watching as a man wearing a bright yellow hard hat and high visibility jacket reached in and removed one of the slips of paper, unfolding it and reading the words written in scribbled handwriting

"Eric Mitchell!" The supervisor called out, his voice echoing back and forth through the factory floor. The process repeated, one name after another was pulled from the cup "Marcus Reed!" the supervisor called out "Alex Mitchel!" Then, when the seventh name was called,

"The new girl!" He yelled, lifting his finger and pointing at Elizabeth, frozen in her place "Claire Black!" he yelled. More hands than she could count wrapped around her arm, passing her from one person to another leading to the front of the room, supervisor leading her the rest of the way with an uncomfortable warm hand on the small of her back. Elizabeth did nothing, watching as she was pushed in front of a table and made to sit down on a cold plastic chair with the number seven placed carelessly on a blue sticker. A shot glass containing a deep brown bitter smelling liquid, the final three names were called.

"Now I know you know the rules," He started, addressing the other workers "but I'm not sure Claire does. Should I explain?" Without waiting for a response he kneeled on the ground, opposite Elizabeth's seat and said, so quiet she barely heard, "It is likely you will die." he whispered, pushing the shot glass towards her, "This glass contains pure Byritherol in liquid form, on the count of ten everyone drinks, last person standing win." Before Elizabeth could ask any more questions he stood up and addressed his captive audience again, yelling louder than before "Do we have any bets?" He asked, quickly adding "Remember the betting tax." Despite this, the crowd roared with bets,

"<Five spunod> on Eric," The first she heard called.

"<Twelve spunod> on Alex," Yelled the second, then someone Elizabeth didn't think would bet did.

"<Seven spunod> on," Danni started "on Claire Black." When voting stopped the supervisor leaned closer and said,

"Looks like you already have a fan." He said, laughing silently to himself, backing away before she could reply. "Ten," He yelled, everyone in the room except Danni and Jane repeating the count down, "Nine!" Elizabeth reached for her mask but stopped, looking over at Jane whose eyes had not left her since she first stepped on the stage. Elizabeth looked over to Danni, who was moving back and forth between her and Jane, Danni followed her look, walking towards Jane. 'Eight!" Danni pushed through the crowd, moving around people and nearly tripping over their feet. "Seven!" Danni reached Jane and just stood there, blocking her view, even from the other side of the room Elizabeth could see her fists clench. '*Keep calm,*' Elizabeth thought. She was too far to hear what was being said. "Six, five, four, three, two" Elizabeth lifted her mask, moving it slightly above her mouth and held it there.

"One!" the audience yelled, watching as all ten downed the drink in one shot, Elizabeth placing her mask over her face as soon as possible. Once she could open her eyes, after the tears had cleared she noticed the beat of heart, pounding in her head like a beast in a cage. A thick fluid ran down her nose then nausea struck, enough to make her consider taking off the mask but she stopped herself. Looking over at Jane who stood there, her hands resting on one of the conveyor belts. Danni's eyes were elsewhere, looking from her to the stairs, to the door they had first entered through.

"Michel down." The supervisor said while she wasn't paying attention, She looked over and saw a man, easily twice her size, lifeless on the floor, being dragged away by men in dungarees a darker colour than everyone else's. Elizabeth looked back at the crowd and found Danni was no longer there. "If you had money on Michel I'm afraid today was not your day." A large portion of the crowd departed, placing small bags on a table, the sound of plastic colliding as the coins hit the table with force. During the next five minutes two people went down and more spunod were placed on the table, some people calmer than others. Now not caring if she was caught, Elizabeth lifted her mask and wiped the sweat off her brow, covering her eyes as the sudden shift in brightness burned them, the smell still hung in her nose.

"You should have said no." At first, it was a voice without a body, definitely feminine with no placeable accent.

"At this point, contestants should start hallucinating, the dose is high enough." Elizabeth looked to her left, people rocking on the spot, hand on head. She looked to the right and everyone was doing the same.

"Up here." The voice repeated, but this time there was a person, her features a mix of European and mediterranean, sitting on a chair similar to the ones Elizabeth sat on but a different colour, a deep shade of crimson red.

Cup of Sleep

"Are you real?" Elizabeth asked, the sound in her head as if she was whispering, the edges of her vision blurring.

"People believed in me." She said, lifting the glass off the table and putting it back down, now full of pills. "People would slaughter livestock and burn precious jewels in my name." She didn't move. "Then they stopped, the gods of old had no power." She picked up the glass again and gave it to Elizabeth.

"What are these?" Elizabeth asked, feeling the plastic-like casing on the pill.

"It's empty." The supervisor said, looking down at her, one eyebrow raised.

"I wasn't talking to you," Elizabeth replied, her words sounding like more of a whisper. The world around her became darker.

"Take the pills and you shall see," Somnus replied. Elizabeth removed one of them and felt it, attempting to separate what looked like two half cases pushed together. A white powder poured out and onto the table, one that didn't have a smell. With closed eyes she raised the glass and drank, the pills entering her mouth with no taste, feeling or smell. A sharp pain erupted through Elizabeth's head as the supervisor said "And Claire is out," then total darkness.

zZZ

5353Andrew James King

Cup of Sleep

She was not there when the bombs dropped, no one currently alive had been with the sole exception of The Glass Lady. A ninety-three-year-old woman who worked for the school board, telling people of the war, of the time nightmares, fell from the sky and took both life and limb. Elizabeth stood in the middle of the road, surrounded by panic and rubble but something else, men on wooden crates stood in the street, megaphone in hand yelling about the progress to be made till their throats were raw. On those crates were the mascot of the Benny Beans corporation, the largest of which was Benny himself and Cydneymon, "*selling coffee*" the box said "*selling the future*." People leaned out of their windows, yelling at the speakers to shut up but they were drowned out by the megaphone.

"Everybody wake up." they yelled, "we have a city to rebuild." Elizabeth stood in the middle of the street, watching as the speakers stepped down from the boxes and, in unison, approached the surrounding houses knocking three times each, all the doors opened at the same time. Elizabeth approached one, seemingly invisible to them

"Good evening," he said, holding out a glass jar full of coffee beans, submerged in the brown liquid she had previously taken a shot of. The knocker removed a

PCM from their pocket and plastic wrapped a styrofoam cup, and poured coffee into it.

"Sorry." the tired speaker said, smelling the overly bitter drink. "I don't like coffee. Can I get back to sleep?" He forced his way into the house, grabbing the woman by the arm and closed the door behind him.

"They came in the night," Somnus spoke, her appearance more translucent than before with complete see through eyes, her voice echoing slightly. "They came for those who refused to drink, those who wanted to rest after the fighting and the chaos."

zZZ

First, she saw the mask, rubber with tinted glass to hide the eyes, then the uniform, dungarees darker than the pair she wore. What she thought was one person seen through double vision was actually two as a man spoke, seeing that her eyes were opening.

"Danni," He said, tapping the other on the arm, "I think she's awake." The woman removed her mask and approached her, resting her hand the glass inches away from Elizabeth's face, the area fogging as Danni sighed through her nose.

"Get her out." She said, walking over to the computer and pressing buttons, the door slid open and

Elizabeth fell out into the waiting arms of the masked figure. Elizabeth looked up and jumped back, slamming her head against the padded back of the sleep pod and stopped, looking over at Danni who was now facing the stranger.

"William," She ordered, "Take your mask off." He obliged, taking off his mask. He appeared to be in his late twenties with short cut ginger facial hair and neatly combed hair of the same colour, his eyes were the greenest Elizabeth had ever seen.

"You must be Elizabeth," He said, holding his hand out for her to shake.

"You must be mistaken." Elizabeth said, taking his hand and gripping it as tight as she could, "My name is Claire Black." Compared to the darkness of his dungarees William's skin seemed paper white. Her eyes darted side to side, stopping occasionally to look at Danni. "Alice," Elizabeth started, looking at the previously masked figure, "Do you know this man?" Danni didn't look up as she searched a green bag.

"Is that your cover name?" He asked, "I hope the actual Alice never finds out." Danni threw the mask, watching as it collided with his chest and fell to the floor .

"It's okay," Danni explained finally, "he works for Matulog."

Cup of Sleep

"Matulog," he repeated, hand over his heart, "searching for Somnus." He lowered himself down, placing Elizabeth's right arm over his shoulder and gesturing for Danni to do the same to the left, an instruction she followed as it was being given.

"Where are we going?" Elizabeth asked, doing her best to keep up with the pair as they walked out of the room and towards the ladder. Elizabeth went first, wrapping her sore hands around each rung of the ladder and lifting herself up, then William and finally Danni climbed, Charlie close behind.

"Eyes forward," William said, causing both Danni and him to laugh.

"You still haven't answered my question," Elizabeth said, watching as the light came closer and closer.

"Oh yeah," William remembered, "near here there's an old house, I'm using it as a base while I'm here." They climbed out of the hole, witnessed by only the birds that flew above the empty street.

Chapter Six
Plant in the Ground

Company Policy Seven-Hundred and Sixteen: If found to be squatting in an abandoned property the coffee supply will be restricted for those involved.

The house in question was an unassuming brick building across the street from the place Elizabeth used to work, unassuming because up until this point she didn't know they existed. Without stopping William walked past both Danni and Elizabeth, unlocking the door and removing his jacket, placing it on a hook next to the door.

"Mi casa, Tu casa." He said, taking the gas masks off the pair and hanging them on the adjacent hooks. Elizabeth walked in, eyes leaping from corner to corner in search of a single red light. "Your friend seems a bit jumpy." He commented, removing from his pocket a small flashlight and pointing it at the corner Elizabeth was currently searching.

"They put cameras in every building," Danni started, "so that if a person dies in private people still know about it and their family can be billed accordingly." She removed from her pocket a ripped slip of paper "Someone delivered this to me yesterday." She explained

"A bill for every bit of coffee and every added flavour Alen had." She inhaled sharply, her eyes trembling, then calmed herself. "It seems the man was a fan of caramel." William took the receipt, unfolded and watched as it fell to his feet. Through the paper Elizabeth could see the number, one million sixteen thousand eight hundred fifty-six cups over twenty- nine years, he was thirty-three when he died. Danni pushed past, walking into the first door and out of sight, both Elizabeth and William followed.

"We have a plan," William said, both of them entering the room which turned out to be the living room.

"Of course you do." Danni said, sitting on the nearest couch and patting the seat next to her "William." She commanded, "Sit." William did as he was told, dragging a small coffee table closer to the seat and placing a USB stick on the glass surface.

"When we found out about Alen's death Alex got worried. Here is a list of people they want to be extracted. Twenty in total" He explained

"Is Alex insane?" Danni exclaimed "They have to know an extraction of that size will be caught." He pointed through the window, through closed blinds, to one of the tallest buildings in the surrounding area. Before he continued Danni's eyes lit up,

"You want to fake their deaths don't you?" She asked, leaning forward, resting her elbows on her knees

5959Andrew James King

and head on her hands. "I had the idea myself but didn't know how to do it." She looked over at Elizabeth "I think I have the right woman." Until that moment Elizabeth hadn't passed the door frame, instead leaning on the door, feeling the handle push into her side. William stood up and approached, holding his hand out.

"Shall we try again?" he asked, his hand on level with hers, "My name is William" he said.

"Elizabeth." She replied, grabbing his hand and shaking it, lighter than last time.

"Why does Danni think you could help?" He asked, moving out of her way, pointing with an open hand at the nearest seat.

"I...I used to work there." Elizabeth explained pointing to the building opposite the house "I was on the twenty-seventh floor, heart attack division." He placed both his hands on Elizabeth's shoulder, laughing.

"You madam," he spoke between great bursts of laughter "are exactly what we have been looking for." His breath smelt weird, lacking the overly bitter or sweet scent of everyone else she had spoken with. In its place was an overly minty scent and strangely white teeth. "Take this," he said, reaching back to the table and picking up the USB stick. "When are you back at work?" he asked, placing the stick in her open palm and closing her fingers around it.

Cup of Sleep

"They think I'm dead." She whispered under her breath, "I can't go back to work." Danni rose from her chair and approached them.

"You may be able to," she satiated, "do you remember that woman, Jane." She said, keeping her distance. "She said there is a report saying you're still alive, she was at the factory looking for you." Elizabeth approached the window, seeing the side of the building and the pile of bodies nearly as tall as the building itself. They were close enough to see corpses at the bottom, maggots and flies clinging to the rotting flesh. Yet they could not smell the decay, instead the strong smell of coffee.

"We need to keep you awake," William said thoughtfully, "going to work perfectly rested will raise suspicion."

"How long will it take?" Danni asked, speaking before Elizabeth could object, Elizabeth sat back down on the couch. Danni left the room, walking through the door and out of the site leaving Elizabeth alone with William. He sat down, crossing his legs as he leaned against the chair next to her, his fingers interlocked.

"How long have you known Danni?" Elizabeth asked, sitting up and facing William.

"We...um," He started "were good friends when we first joined Matulog. Haven't seen each other in a while though." Danni returned, breaking the silence that hung in the air like coffee fumes and made a request. "Could you two get the sleep pod?" She asked both Elizabeth and William, leaning against the door, a mug emitting steam in her hand.

"How are we supposed to bring it here?" Elizabeth countered, "It's underground in a different building." Danni removed from her pocket a set of keys and threw them to Elizabeth who caught them between her fingers.

"These are the keys to my house," she explained. "In the basement where you first found the pod there's a tunnel to the factory. Go through there." Before questions could be asked she pushed past, out of the living room and into the hallway, Elizabeth stood there, watching as she descended the stairs into the basement.

zZZ

"You first," William stated, pointing at the door, Elizabeth did as she was told, followed closely by William as they stepped onto the street, greeted first by the coldness of the air and then by a slamming sound as another body was added to the pile. The body not settling at the top but instead rolling down and landing at the foot of the stack, blood pooling around the scared face. "Why don't they clean that up?" William asked

"They say it's too big to do anything about," Elizabeth answered.

"What about earlier?" William asked, "before it got so high." Without saying anything Elizabeth approached the body and grabbed its arm, flipping it over and using her hand to wipe away the blood. William lept back, covering his mouth with his hand to hide how close he was to being sick. "Is that?" He asked, wiping his mouth with his sleeve.

"Yes," Elizabeth confirmed. "It's Alen." saying no more Elizabeth dragged him along the ground, through the empty street to the park, every bit of metal was rusted, every side was full of holes and every wooden bench was rotten.

"What are you doing?" William asked, "Danni's house is that way." He was pointing in the opposite direction, away from where Elizabeth was dragging the body.

"Do you have a shovel?" Elizabeth asked, resting the body on the largest patch of dirt.

"You want to bury him don't you?" William asked "Why do you want to do that?"

"Danni is grieving," she explained, pointing in a random direction she hoped the house was, "She had lost her husband and her daughter." Without speaking, his hand resting against his forehead, he walked off, back the direction they came and towards the house. Elizabeth sat on the floor, silently wiping Alens face with her sleeve, cleaning it off mud, blood and dust. Minutes later William returned, shovel in one hand, folding chair in the other.

"Have a seat," he commanded, unfolding the chair and resting the tip of the shovel in the earth before pushing it through with a sturdy stomp on the step of the shovel.

"Did you know Alen?" Elizabeth asked, looking at the keys she was given.

William paused for a moment then replied. "He was, um… my romantic rival." Elizabeth leaned forward, resting her chin on her hand. "Alen and I both liked Danni," He explained, lifting piles of dirt out of the ground and gently tossing it next to him.

"Any grand romantic gestures?" Elizabeth asked curiously.

"What?" William asked puzzled, the pace of his digging slowed, "Like a date?"

"No," Elizabeth corrected, "I mean did you write poems? Did you give a romantic speech? Was there music?" William stabbed the shovel into the ground, groaning and he sat next to it on the bone dry dirt.

"There was a poem." He answered reluctantly, causing Elizabeth to laugh, her eyes filling with tears.

Cup of Sleep

"I bet it was awful," She teased.

"I'll have you know," he countered, "I'm a poet and a romantic." He removed from his pocket a sheet of folded brown paper and spoke its contents aloud.

"D is for desire, a face on which any painter could retire
A is for adore, a laugh that leaves me wanting more
N is for never, the time I will leave you forever.
N is for noble, with a heart and soul which should be global
I is for I love you, a fact that shall always be true."

Elizabeth continued laughing yet at the same time she spoke "What does that even mean?" She asked.

"I don't know," he replied "I was eighteen and madly in love." He stood up and continued digging, talking at the same time. "You must have done something like that." Elizabeth silently shook her head, "Anyone do something like that to you?" He was still digging, the pile and dirt up to his ankle.

"Not that I remember." Elizabeth replied "I liked people but they never liked me back." He stopped digging, the pile now up to his shin, and offered her the shovel, she took it without complaining and they swapped places.

"I doubt that," He countered.

"Why?" She asked.

Cup of Sleep

"You have pleasant facial features," He explained "I'm surprised no one saw it." Elizabeth continued digging.

"A face on which any painter could retire?" she asked, laughing but slower due to the effort of digging and the weight of the dirt.

"I'm never gonna hear the end of that, am I?" he asked, his voice accompanied by a long sigh, yet laughter followed.

"It will stop when you leave her forever," She replied. The annoyance melted away and left behind only a deep laughter. Then silence for an hour, During that hour the shovel swapped hands seven times, both Elizabeth and William digging Alen's grave.

"Would you say that's deep enough?" He asked, placing his foot into the ground, looking at the surrounding dirt which now rose to his upper thigh

"I think so," Elizabeth replied. William stood up and approached the body, grabbing the legs. Without words Elizabeth understood. She approached the body, looping her arms under his shoulders and lifting, quickly moving the body to the side and, as gently as they could, lowered it into the freshly dug grave. William took the shovel and began replacing the dirt with the speed and efficiency of one who had done this before and knew he would do it again.

"Should I get Danni?" William asked.

"No," Elizabeth replied, "I have a plan," She smiled softly.

"What is that plan?" He questioned

"I'm getting Sarah, her body I mean," She answered, "the Danvis Family will be buried here." He stood at the head of the grave for a moment of silence, a single tear rolled down his face and splashed onto the freshly dug dirt.

"I'm sorry for your loss," Elizabeth consoled, "You two must have been good friends." He lifted his shirt, showing a long cut on his side from upper thigh to below his ribs

"The guy was a fan of swashbuckling romance," He explained, "challenged me to a duel and won."

"Is that how he ended up with Danni?" Elizabeth questioned.

"No," He answered "This was a few days into deployment here, I was telling him to use the sleep pod but he refused, saying it needed to look realistic." Without another word the pair faced away from the grave, shovel still buried in the earth and left the park, Danni's keys clinking in Elizabeth's pocket.

Chapter Seven
After Taste

Company Policy Three-Hundred and Eighty-Five: Anyone who returns a supply of tea greater than twelve bags shall be entitled to a reward of <two-hundred> spunods for every six bags.

With shaky hands Elizabeth inserted the key into the lock, turning it , sighing as the door clicked and swung open. They removed all of the furniture from her house, the stairs ahead of them no longer covered by a carpet just dust coated wood.

"Where is this tunnel?" William asked, blocking his nose with both his hands.

"Through here," Elizabeth directed, pointing to the staircase that lead to the basement, both their breaths could be seen in the cold air, the area around Elizabeth's eye felt dry. "Be careful," Elizabeth warned, placing her hand against William's chest to stop him moving any further.

"What's wrong?" He asked.

"There could be cameras now."

"But there weren't any before?"

"That was before the police raided her house and found she was an unproductive."

Cup of Sleep

"Is that honestly what they call people who sleep?" He asked bewildered

"Yes, because when you sleep you can't help recover from the war," Elizabeth explained. He looked out the door, eyes scanning the buildings that, while not in the best shape, stood with a look of wellness often not seen in those struck by a bomb.

"It looks like you recovered long ago," he stated. The pair walked further into the house, keeping an eye on the corner of the house for a blinking red light.

"I saw her," Elizabeth said abruptly.

"Who?"

"Somnus, back in the factory. She was sitting on the table when I took the shot of Byritherol."

"Was she actually there?" He asked.

"My point is there's something in the coffee, something that causes hallucinations. The sleep pod must have gotten it out of my system."

"What did she tell you?" He asked

"She showed me about the time before sleep was outlawed. I was in the middle of a street, there were people standing on boxes yelling about how we need to recover." They descended the stairs, William ducking to protect his head from the low ceiling. Silently they walked, feeling the edge of the ill lit room till they came across an empty bookshelf. A small amount of air flowing through the gap between it and the wall. Using the tips of their fingers, Elizabeth on the right and William on the left, they both pulled. They jumped backwards to avoid the dusty shelves landing on their feet. On the other side there was darkness, a tunnel so absent of light that, as they ran their hands along the jagged, damp walls, it seemed as though they had closed their eyes.

"Are you still there?" Elizabeth asked, William simply shushed her, walking at a pace only slightly slower than Elizabeth so he had to stop occasionally and let her progress further "Do you think anyone can hear us?" Elizabeth continued. They pushed through the gap, chunks of the wall breaking off as their hand rested temporarily on the jagged points.

"We are entering a coffee factory," He explained in a hushed voice, "through a path we cannot see. Anyone could be on the other side." They saw a light at the end, temporarily cut off by a passing shadow, they continued, using the corner to pull themselves out, gasping as the tightness around their ribs and stomach loosened.

"This is big." A voice from the other side of the wall spoke, "there got to be some sort of reward for that, a sleep pod."

"Not just a sleep pod," a different voice explained, "the sleep pod. The final sleep pod." Elizabeth leaned around the door, looking into the large chamber and seeing two men, feet up on the table, eating cereal and drinking cups of strong smelling coffee.

"Not just a sleep pod," the first person spoke through his gas mask, "but tea as well. Do you know the last time someone found a supply of tea? Even one this small." The bags were scattered on the table, a few falling on the floor as they adjusted their feet, placing the foot that was once on top at the bottom.

"That's why we need to keep this quiet," the second explained, "at least until we can tell the boss." Elizabeth opened her mouth to speak but Willaim was quicker, stepping the length of the door frame and pushing her against the wall, one hand over her mouth and the other against the back of her head to cushion the impact against the wall.

"We need a plan," he whispered, he pulled away and resumed their previous positions. A beep sound could be heard, followed by the sound of a hot, bitter smelling liquid being poured into a ceramic cup, a bang as their masks were placed on a part of the table uncovered by tea bags, and took a drink, downing the still steaming liquid. They placed their PCD back on the table and went back to the sleep pod, opening it and feeling the soft padding at the back. William reached into his pocket and removed a case, two circles with a plastic eye drop containing a clear liquid. He opened one of the circles and picked something small and transparent out of the box, his eyes going from well rested to those of a man who hadn't lept in more weeks than he had fingers on his hands. "Hold this," He requested, giving Elizabeth the case. She did what he said, taking the case out of his and holding it. He removed something else from the case and with one hand he held Elizabeth's eye open, using the other to place the thing into her eye causing it to water up. Elizabeth removed from her pocket a small hand mirror, her eyes marked by bags that seemed to get darker the further down she looked.

"What's the plan?" Elizabeth asked.

"Follow my lead," He instructed. He quickly stepped through the door frame and approached the table, taking from it one of the PCDs.

"Get your hands off that," one of the men spoke, his mask off revealing pale skin which contrasted the pitch black of his walrus moustache. Elizabeth followed William's actions, picking the other PCD holding her hand over the button.

"What are you doing?" The other asked, swiping at Elizabeth trying to get it back, she raised her hand, her thumb accidentally pressing the button and causing some of the liquid to pour out.

"No!" he exclaimed, attempting again to reach for the PCD. "Don't do that!" William held the button for just a second, watching as half a cup of coffee fell from the device.

"Sit down." William instructed, a calm intimidation making Elizabeth herself almost listen.

"Not until you give us them back!" the first man demanded, his friend having already taken his seat. William held the button again, watching as another half a cup fell from the device, the burning liquid splashing at his feet, yet his face showed no pain. The first man lowered himself onto the chair covering his eyes with his hands. William looked at the side of the PCD in Elizabeth hand and, without saying anything he nodded, holding his hand out waiting for Elizabeth to give it to him, she did, placing the device in his hand and walking over to the sleep pod, looking around the lower half for wheels, kicking the lock which stopped it from rolling.

"I've got it," Elizabeth confirmed. William took both devices, holding down the buttons and watched all of of the liquid poured out at once, the two men attempting to leap over the table, dragging themselves along it on their stomach as the liquid poured,

Beep beep beep

The sound emerged from the PCDs causing all others to cease. The first man grabbed William by the shirt and began lowering to the floor, his final words mumbled under his breath as slowly his eyes closed.

7373Andrew James King

Cup of Sleep

"We prepare our brew
For the very tired few
Sugar packs we pour
Never more than four
For Benny do we live
For Benny, do we Drink."

His last breath was visible in the cold of the abandoned chamber where not even the cameras worked. The other man had died without words, his head slumped lower than his shoulders, his forehead rested against the tea bag covered table.

"Why did you do that?" Elizabeth asked, pulling the man to the floor and placing her hand on his sweaty neck, feeling the absence of a pulse.

"They saw your face, they saw our faces." He reached up to his right eye, holding it open with one hand and using the other to push the small lens to the corner of his eye, folding it and pulling it out of his eye, he did the same with his left eye.

"Put them in the sleep pod!" Elizabeth yelled. "Like Danni did with me."

"Can you guarantee they won't report us?" He asked.

Cup of Sleep

"No I can't," She replied, "But we should have tried."

"Why did you change your mind?" He asked, genuine curiosity marking his voice.

"I'm the reason Sarah is dead," she mumbled, so quiet she barely heard herself

"What did you say?" He asked. Tears began streaming down her face.

"Sarah is dead because of me!" She yelled, turning around and wiping her eyes with her sleeve, leaving a red damp mark on her eyelids.

"It wasn't your fault," William countered, "Danni told me what happened. The police killed her."

"Why do you think the police were there?"

"Because Jane told them about the sleep pod."

"How do you think Jane knew about the sleep pod?" He placed one hand on each of Elizabeth's shoulders and turned her around so they looked eye to eye despite the height difference.

"If you keep thinking like that," He scolded, "you could blame everyone for everything. Trust me, it wasn't your fault."

"Ok." she replied just wanting the conversation to end. Silently she approached the pod, using one hand to push the top down and the bottom forward. They rolled the pod through the tunnel, sweat dripped down Elizabeth's brow as they pushed, barely fitting the pod through the tight gap that seemed bigger now than it was, sections of the wall appearing to push back as they approached, leaving behind sharp stones on the ground which both Elizabeth and William stood on. Reaching the staircase Elizabeth grabbed the top and William grabbed the bottom, lifting the pod off the ground by enough distance to clear the narrow staircase and finally onto flat land.

"Can you take this back to the house?" Elizabeth asked, "I need to get something." They parted ways, Elizabeth walking towards the call of birds.

Chapter Eight
Thought and Memory

Company Policy Fourteen: Till the age of fourteen you will remain in an unproductive education facility where they will be taught the truth behind the burden that is sleep

Ravens circled the house and Elizabeth as she approached, resting on a nearby fence, their glassy eyes following her hand as she picked up a nearby rock and removed the spare key from an indent in the bottom. One of them flew over, landing on her arm and resting its talons into her skin, the cold pain spreading through her arm causing her to jump back, but the bird remained its head tilting side to side as Elizabeth whispered.

"Hello," Rubbing one finger up and down its cold beak. Without warning it flew off, its wings slapping Elizabeth as it took flight. Elizabeth slid the key into the lock, feeling the click as she turned it and pushed, greeted by the ruin and decay of a house untouched for two decades. First there were the cobwebs, the instinctive waving of her hands as the dusty webs covered her face and hair, then the smell, a smell of decay that felt somehow old and new as if someone had died here recently.

Cup of Sleep

"Is anyone here?" she called, passing through the
door and into the living room. "Mrs. Vanderhep?" Again
she saw a raven, pecking at the wood of the bannister, the
once white railing now the brownish green colour of
rotting wood. Approaching the stairs, moving her hand
closer to her body to avoid the bannister. She reached the
top of the stairs and was faced with a door, one she slowly
grasped the handle of, breathing slowly as she turned and
opened it. The room was full of beds, eight small beds
without mattresses pushed up against the wall, four on
each side with a bedside cabinet and a lamp and blue bulb
which flickered on and off at inconsistent intervals. On a
table at the opposite side of the room Elizabeth saw a
small statue of a woman, with no arms, on the base of
which was a screen that had been off for over a decade. It
was here she was raised. Starting life as a kicking baby
ripped from the arms and gaze of her mother. It was here
she spent her last night as a child. Then she was kicked
out, left on the street on the day of her fourteenth birthday.
Her only gift that year was the PCD that was her first but
definitely not her last. Elizabeth wrapped her hand around
the statue and twisted, listening as the neck popped off,
separating from the body with more force than she
expected. Out poured pills, small and white with a plastic
feeling on which the familiar smell clung that once filled
her mind with the will to continue, to rebuild. Yet now the

Andrew James King

Cup of Sleep

smell of coffee reminded her of the beating of her heart, how it could stop at any moment. Almost out of instinct she reached for back pocket, checking for her PCD, her heart rate increasing when she felt nothing but the denim of the dungarees and the thin layer of dirt which clung to them. Elizabeth lay on one of the beds, feeling each individual board press into her back at inconsistent distances apart. She lay facing the lamp every impulse telling her to pick it up and throw it out the window; instead she took the pills in hand and threw them at the bulb watching as they bounced off the glass which wasn't even scratched by the force. She closed her eyes and, in spite of everything around trying to prevent it, let sleep embrace her, its warm arms leading her to a dream.

zZZ

'It was quiet' Elizabeth thought as she sat up in the body of her younger self, the room now full of life silent yet ever present. Then slowly, as if emerging from water, the music began playing, a slow repetitive tune of high pitched noise which hung in her ear. Even when the wind up key of the music box stopped playing. The figure known as Mrs. Vanderhep passing her vision as she approached the

small marble like statue of Somnus to turn the handle, the music played again

"What's up with her?" The whisper echoed through the room with no point of origin, a group of five children chin rested on the palms of their hands as they stared in her direction.

"It's her fourteenth birthday." the originless whisper replied. Mumbling followed, unhearable words passed from child to child as they sat up higher and higher and once they could get no higher they stood up. Their eyes marked by the grey bags of sleeplessness despite the eight hours a night lay in bed. The switch to the light keeping them awake buried in the centre of a transparent case. Pain flared in her cheek, three lines running sharply across which felt as though they drew blood but the only liquid she found there was tears she did not know she was shedding. A hand wrapped around her wrist, lifting her frail body off the bed with the same ease she lifted the styrofoam cup, she was dragged across the floor her knees brushing against splinters of wood, loose stone and the hot stains of recently spilled coffee as the chanting behind her became audible

"Unproductive." Came the whisper as she was dragged across the floor and down the stairs each drop more painful than the last as the jolt caused the non-existent drop on her cheek to drop quicker and quicker, to her it felt like each hit was pushing her knee cap out of place. Elizabeth looked up, seeing on the collar of her shirt a brooch, the image within being a black coffee bean contrasting the black background made of the same marble looking plastic as the music box.

"Stop!" She yelled as she reached the bottom of the stairs, yet the dragging did not stop. Around the corner and into an office sparse of decoration, just a table, two chairs and a coffee maker. Mrs. Vanderhep produced from the machine two styrofoam cups filled near to the brim with the steaming brown liquid that kept them both awake and alive.

"Drink" Mrs. Vanderhep Demanded as she pushed the drink closer to her, half the cup hanging over the edge but not falling. Elizabeth took a sip. She remembered hating it, the dry feeling it left as she swallowed the burning liquid, the strength of the flavour which left her eyes watering. All the while the pain in her cheek got worse and worse like a blade running across the flesh on her face drawing blood that did not flow. Mrs. Vanderhep added a coffee spoon full of sugar and mixed it in. "This is important," Mrs. vanderhep instructed, watching as Elizabeth took another sip, coughing as the drink was still too bitter. Another spoonful of sugar was added to the cup and mixed till it dissolved in the liquid.

Cup of Sleep

"How long did you sleep last night?" Mrs. Vanderhep questioned, waiting for a response by drinking her cup.

"An hour," Elizabeth replied under her breath.

"What's wrong?" Vanderhep asked, using her forefinger to lift Elizabeth's head, her eyes scanned the room from side to side.

"I've seen her." Elizabeth whispered "In my dreams." Using the whole of her hand Vanderhep grabbed Elizabeth by the wrist and pulled her closer,

"Speak child, speak," Elizabeth felt disgusted by the strong smell of coffee which marked Vanderhep's every breath, her teeth stained brown with years of drinking the bitter substance. "What is she doing!?" She demanded loudly.

"She speaks to me." Elizabeth replied. "Tells me secrets." She began frantically trying to remove her hand from the older woman's grasp, each pull hurting more than the last.

"When did this start?" She demanded again, getting even closer than before her bloodshot eyes against Elizabeth with less than an inch between them.

"I don't know." Elizabeth whisper shouted with a hoarse voice, using her free hand to wipe from her face both tears and spit which flew from the mouth of the woman yelling about her dreams.

8282Andrew James King

Cup of Sleep

"Do not lie to me girl." Her false teeth shifted in her mouth. With as much strength as she could muster, Elizabeth pulled arm back, finally freeing it from the grasp of the old woman's hand, the bonyness of her fingers sending a shiver down Elizabeth's spine. Raising to full height she yelled.

"Don't call me that." but the height was short lived as the force from the back of Vanderhep's hand sent her tumbling to the ground. Her hands were not quick enough to catch her so for a moment her sight was nothing more than a blur of colours. A near imperceivable blur moved behind Vanderhep, a woman in a suit appeared over her shoulder watching. yet the pain in her cheek still stood out, a short thin line that felt as if it might bleed at any second. Vanderhep stood with fists raised, two clenched hands which seemed like the spiked ends of maces raised above Vanderhep's head, she awoke before they made impact.

$$zZZ$$

Before she knew what was going on she felt his arms, his cool hand resting against the dripping sweat on her forehead, he was cradling her yet she could not see his face, she didn't care.

"It's okay." The voice of William spoke as his grip softened, but remained, Elizabeth felt lightheaded.

"She's here." She whispered "Vanderhep and the children." She stood up, moving from bed to bed looking under each, finding no sign of other life. William seemed hesitant, his hand hovered hesitantly over Elizabeth's shoulder. "I saw them," Elizabeth cried. "They were here, where have they gone?"

"I don't know what you mean," He explained, "we're the only people here." Elizabeth stood up and approached the closet, placing her hands on the handles and breathing deeply through her nose. "What are you doing?" William asked.

"They're always in closets." She said, half her mind pulling at the doors, the other screaming to not wake the beast.

"What's always in the closet?" He asked.

"The monsters." Elizabeth answered using every ounce of her self control to look calm "we were told they make a mockery of productivity. Walking and talking yet sleeping, doing nothing." William sighed

"And do these monstrosities have a name?" He asked, placing his hand on the gap on the handles under mine.

"Sleepwalkers." Elizabeth whispered, William's reaction the opposite of what she was expecting as he began laughing, "it's not funny." She exclaimed, elbowing his chest "it is said they're the puppets of Somnus." before she could react she felt a push on the door, they slid open dsite her protest

"I present the sleepwalker." William said. The door swung open with both a pulling and pushing force as something fell from the closet, pushing the pair to the floor, Elizabeth's head hitting against William's chest as on top of the pair lay a skeleton, bones brown with rot, upon lump of that was once a shirt stood a brooch the image within the silhouette of a coffee bean, black against the mabel looking white background. A muffled sound emerged from behind Elizabeth as Willaim screamed, the sound trapped behind his sealed lips and trembling hands. Elizabeth lifted the remains, the heavy feeling of the bones pushing against her wrist causing her to grunt as they pushed it to arms length and finally to the side, its empty eye sockets staring at the pair as they stumbled to their feet.

"Who the hell is that?" William whispered, using his foot to roll it onto its back.

"I-I think," Elizabeth stuttered "I think it's Vanderhep."

"Who?" William asked as he climbed over the bed, getting closer to the door sticking to the opposite wall to avoid the remains, Elizabeth followed in similar manner, her back pushed uncomfortably close to the bedframe and across the matressless bottoms.

"She ran this Sleep education centre. Making sure the beds were uncomfortable, reading the more impressionable children horror stories, that sort of thing."

"Why?"

"They didn't just want us to ignore sleep, they wanted us to fear it." Elizabeth picked up the music box, taking it with her as they passed through the doorway and into a passing silent crowd, the centre of which held a large crate each hand passing it further and further to the front. The celebration of Boston Harbour was about to begin.

Chapter Nine
Spill The Tea

Company Policy eight-hundred and twenty seven: On the second Tuesday of every month shall the noble sacrifice of the men from Boston for their freedom be celebrated by the repetition of their actions, the releasing of tea into a harbour.

Through the crowd Elizabeth ran, followed slowly by William weaving between people who locked hands, carrying in their mouth with a look of disgust, tea bags of various shapes. Square, triangle and circle. For miles the line stretched, people shambling through the streets each footstep in unison like each stepper was chained together at the ankle yet each of their faces were decorated by a weak, shaky smile from the back of the crowd to the front. Elizabeth followed suit, grasping the nearest unclaimed hand in her right and William's with her left, a distant voice saying

"It can't be." as they marched. Then the crowd stopped, each row at a time moved their foot for the last time and paused, all faces pointed in the same direction, towards a stage upon which stood a man, his visage half shrouded in a mask the colour of coffee lightened by cream, the upper half of his face exposed.

"Do you trust me?" Elizabeth asked, parting before William could reply and pushing herself to the front of the crowd, her fingertips brushing against the stage. Close enough to hear the static pouring through the otherwise silent speakers. The masked figure took the microphone and held it to his mouth.

"Ladies and gentlemen," his speech began. "I don't think I need to tell you who we're here to honour." As he began speaking, rising and lowering his voice to be heard over the cheering crowd "the brave men and women of seventeen seventy-three." As he continued Elizabeth walked around to the side, passed a guard whose eyes were blocked by his coffee based cup. Once she got past him Elizabeth felt and half grasp her wrist, dragging her to the side behind the curtains that hid the recording equipment and stage props, everyone so distracted that they didn't notice when two people who didn't belong appeared from a curtain that should be guarded.

"What are you planning?" William asked, releasing her arm and sitting down on a box. Elizabeth reached into a box and pulled out a machete, its serrated blade looking more like teeth than a simple knife. "No." Was all Willaim said, seeing his face reflected in the freshly polished metal.

Cup of Sleep

"Yes." was all Elizabeth replied as with a sadistic grin on her face she walked through the curtain sitting at the top of the rickety wooden stairs listening to the speech she had heard everyday.

"And out into the harbour poured the cursed powder, the eternal symbol of oppression that we have been free of for near a hundred years. Tea." A chorus of boos, hisses and tears emerged from the crowd at the mere mention of the word, Elizabeth barely managing to contain herself as the man spoke on and on about the vile liquid and freedom, "so now I present." the man said, gesturing towards the teabags as Elizabeth stood up and approached the man, raising the machete above her head and swinging down

"I'm still alive!" she yelled as her sharp blade sliced through the spout of the container causing the tea to pour out into the harbour. There was a moment, a brief silence during which all eyes were on her, their tired gaze dropping occasionally only to shoot back up less than a second later, Jane was the first person to speak. Yelling which could be heard over the intense silence of the countless rows that separated the two.

"Elizabeth," the called as she pushed through the crowd, not caring about the many toes she stood on or the people she pushed out of the way as she approached the stage, stopping with the tips of her fingers resting on the

8989Andrew James King

edge of stage which stood on level with her neck, a knowing smile spread across her face.

"It has been a while." Elizabeth said as she held out her arm to lift Jane off the ground and onto the stage.

"They'll be here any second." Jane whispered, her warm, coffee scented breath uncomfortably close to Elizabeth's neck.

"Who?" Elizabeth asked. Before she could answer they arrived, their uniform militaristic in every way except the aprons which hung loosely around their necks not even tied around the back.

"Unproductive, kneel down with your hands behind your back." with one hand Jane pushed Elizabeth back, holding her other hand in the air between her and the guards.

"She's not an unproductive, there's been a misunderstanding." Jane yelled as they walked around the stage ignoring her.

"Drop the machete." They commanded and obeyed, having forgotten what she was holding but wincing as the blade stuck into the ground mere centimetres away from her foot, burying a part of the freshly sharpened blade in the ground.

"You have to understand," Jane tried explaining "she was kidnapped, forced to use a sleep pod against her will." They approached from behind, pressing a metal tube into her arm which produced three needles filling her veins with a cold liquid which rushed through her body, her eyes widened and her heart beat, faster and louder. So loud that she could barely hear the voices around her, beating like a drum in her mind, her legs became numb beneath her as Jane rested her hand on the back of Elizabeth's neck, slowly lowering her to the ground, the sudden shift from the hot air to the cold ground causing her to shiver. "All will be made clear," Jane whispered, "and then you can be productive like the rest of us." Darkness.

$$zZZ$$

She did not dream during that slumber, her eyes showing her nothing, she heard only footsteps as the armoured men approached, their dry, shaking hands resting under her shoulders and knees from which she was lifted up and placed on a stretcher. She still heard their voices as they rested her on the stretcher and spoke.

"Is this Elizabeth?" one of them asked, the voice sounding from her legs, "the one who's been missing?"

"Yes," the one standing next to her confirmed. She felt the pain as they dropped her, the pain flaring from the back of her head hitting the ground, the blaring sound of their beepers overwhelming all other sounds and all at once they collapsed to the ground, the thud so close to Elizabeth's head that she flinched.

"We need more security!" Jane called out as a similar yet quieter thud sounded as something shattered next to her head, the broken shards of glass of a PCD resting on her cheek. Hearing no other sound, but feeling herself being lifted off the ground, she was carried away not where she was going or who was taking her there.

zzZ

The smell of coffee, the heat and the silence were overwhelming. That was the first thing Elizabeth realised after she opened her eyes, slowly at first and then all at once, the sudden transition from darkness into the light near blinding her.

"Made you a cup of coffee." the voice from the other side of the table declared "according to Jane this is how you like it." At first she didn't drink it, instead lifting the mug and running her finger around the rim. Her vision cleared and soon she saw the one who had spoken, their face covered by a gas mask which was a silhouette against the bright light which crept around the edge of their body.

Cup of Sleep

"Too much milk," Elizabeth complained after a small sip of the drink before her, the hand so small she could not pick it up without burning her finger.

"What did she say?" was the first thing they asked

"I'm sorry," Elizabeth told the figure than now seemed closer than before, "what did who say?" wordlessly they removed from their pocket a phone, on which was playing a video of a police car stopping outside a coffee shop and not long after, easily less than a minute, Elizabeth followed.

"Did Mrs. Davis tell you anything?" the figure asked

"lies and propaganda."she replied "nonsense about Benny being evil, and sleep being important. You know the filth they think." she heard gulping as through the lifted mask they drank a full cup of coffee.

"Did you overhear any of her plans?" The figure asked as soon as the coffee cup thudded against the table, the sound marked by an almost exaggerated sigh of relief. Elizabeth paused, the plan sitting at the tip of her tongue, her old life just a few words away.

"They're planning an attack." she said, her interrogator sitting up straight in their chair, their expression unreadable due to the mask, "They're gonna bomb the cinnamon factory." the figure slouched, the sudden panicked jump seeming to have never happened.

9393Andrew James King

"What do they plan on using?" The figure took out a pen and notepad, taking a brief note of what she said.

"They have a bomb," she told them, "I heard they plan on placing it in with one of the shipments and detonating it as soon as they know it's there. They think it's gonna kill fifty-six people." She dived across the table, stopping only when the cuffs that held her to the metallic surface had reached their maximum length, slamming her nose against the table. From behind mask Elizabeth could hear laughing, the figures' shoulders rising and falling at an ever quickening pace.

"I almost believed you." the figure said, rising slowly to their feet and circling the table, "Even though I know more about the real plan than you do." standing at full height, reaching into the darkness, sparks appeared from the corner briefly lighting it before disappearing. "I think you're ready." they said, their hand resting on the lower half of their mask.

"But you caught me lying?" Elizabeth asked

"No I didn't," Danni replied, resting her mask on the table, "you lied through your teeth and believed you." next to the mask she put the camera she had removed from the wall.

"What are you doing here?" Elizabeth asked, barely stopping herself yelling as she heard the footsteps of guards passing the door, not stopping or slowing as they passed.

"I wish I could explain this in less hostile circumstances but you sort of forced my hand. She removed from her pocket a napkin, the brown figure of Cydneymon decorating the corners, a list of ten names

> Evie-May Schaefer
> Nevaeh Rubio
> Killian Sparrow
> Adrienne Gilliam
> Esther Weston
> Mariam Greer
> Ramsha Rodriguez
> Waseem Roman
> Aleena Freeman
> Ioan Bowler

"These are half the agents that need to be declared dead, the circumstance of their deaths should appear suspicious," she folded the paper again and placed it back in her pocket, "you will be sent to investigate which is exactly what we want and where you fit in, we need you to confirm the narrative, whatever it may be. Welcome to Matulog, searching for Somnus." She placed the mask over her head, tightening the straps and walking towards the door, resting her hand on the hand and pushing it down.

"What will you be doing?" Elizabeth asked

Cup of Sleep

"I have some deaths to fake," she answered as she pushed the door open, two similarly dressed guards walking through and pulling her out of her chair. "We are both gonna need some seriously good luck." she said before disappearing on the other side.

"Mr. Rincword would like a word with you," one of the guards explained, "In his office." They lead her through the hall, around uncountable corridors and into the main office, Jane tiredly waving at her from her desk, she made her way to his office, the holes that once lined the walls without letting wind in were no longer there, just the cheerful eyes of Benny and the words. A good citizen has already beaten Somnus.

Chapter Ten
A Productive morning

Company policy sixty-eight: Any time taken away from your desk for the purposes of eating or reliving one's self will be deducted from pay, rounded up to the nearest hour.

Harold Rincword rubbed his eyes, the redness and the puffiness so extreme that Elizabeth thought it was a miracle he could see, but it was clear that he could as she entered through the silent door and approached the chair facing him.

"Sounds like you had an unproductive day." He said, pausing to drink to his side, hitting his chest as the steaming liquid flowed through him. Elizabeth did the same, hesitant as she lifted the cup and drank, first sipping then as the caffeine and Byritherol hit she downed the whole thing, she could feel the world warp around her as, for a second, she saw a hole appear in the wall, a hole which let no wind through closing as quickly as it opened.

"You start back at work as soon as possible, how about in an hour?" Elizabeth went to open her mouth to speak but as soon as Harold saw this his fist slammed into the table yelling "You do not open your mouth." While shaking his hand "nod for yes and shake your head for no! Do you understand?!"

Elizabeth nodded

"Do you want to return to work today?"

Elizabeth nodded.

9797Andrew James King

"Did talking to the unproductives influence you in any way?"

Elizabeth shook her head

"Would you like to sit at your old desk?"

Elizabeth nodded.

"Next to Jane?"

Elizabeth shook her hand, feeling her heart beat in her head.

"Too bad!" he yelled again, his fist causing the wood of the table to creek under the force. "She will be your supervisor as you investigate more deaths. We need to make sure what happened to you doesn't happen again. Do you understand!"

Elizabeth nodded

"There has been a massive backlog of deaths on your log since your disappearance. Get to it!" he yelled as a dismissal, watching as Elizabeth stood off her chair and approached the door, using her shoulder to open it before hearing Harold call her name. Elizabeth nodded

"Speak!" He yelled across the room.

"Yes sir." she said, her back propping the heavy door open.

"Go to reception and get your new PCD." Elizabeth closed the door behind her, leaning against it and taking a moment, however brief, to sit in the silence and Harold's shouting failed to interrupt her peace.

"You must be Elizabeth." the receptionist said, standing over her with the PCD held at arm's length, a hesitant untrusting look on her face.

Cup of Sleep

"You must be Harold's assistant." Elizabeth replied.

"Sarah." she replied "but most people call me Sar" Elizabeth took the PCD from her hand, thanking her, and stood off the door. "he's not always like that." she said "he's not always angry." without replying Elizabeth walked down the hall, past the paintings of former managers which hung on the walls with eyes that followed her every stop, their still painted lips saying one thing without moving till she reached the end, just before the the empty frame that will one day hold the visage of Harold, what once was the face of his predecessor, was now a plank canvas, an x across it the brown of coffee.

"We know what you did." Elizabeth was nervous as she pushed through the worn wood of the door which divided the office from the manager's department and looked over her co-workers, listening to the click of every key as the workers typed away, their every move under the watchful eye of Benny.

"Elizabeth!" a voice cried from beside her desk "I'm glad you're okay!" Elizabeth approached Jane, keeping as much of a distance as possible as her co-worker spoke. "what happened?" Elizabeth sat at her desk and began typing, pulling up the names of the people she would need to sort out.

"Can you please Just leave me alone?" Elizabeth asked, quickly turning her chair around and looking Jane in the eyes before turning again to face the computer.

Name: Christopher Smith
Gender: Male (he/him)
Age: 28
Address: 3 Eden Close, Hucknall",NG15 6SR
Cause of death: Coffee Withheld by members of Matulog
Notes: members that caused this death are unknown, be careful

She looked over the information, the picture of the man's face which seemed familiar, his hands sliding down William's shirt as the words she had known from birth crept from his lips.

"Did you see what I did?" Jane asked, resting her arms on the divide between their desks "about the unproductives that captured you?"

"Yes I did." Elizabeth answered before turning back to her computer and finishing her work, pressing print on the computer and listening to the buzz of the printer beneath her desk as it dispensed the receipt., five minutes passed, the repeated low buzz in the back of her mind seeming endless.

"She was shot right in the face!" again using her fingers as guns.

"Could you please be quiet?" Elizabeth asked, taking a sip of the coffee which she poured from her new PCD.

Cup of Sleep

"You should be happy." Jane said "another unproductive off the street. A cause for celebration." Jane drank her coffee like water, neither the heat of the liquid nor the caffeine having any effect on her. "Do you remember your first unproductive?" She asked, Elizabeth nodded.

Name: Josephine May
Gender: Female (she/her)
Age: 19
Address: 20 East Parade, Baildon",BD17 6LY
Cause of death: underfilled PCD
Note: collect PDC to prevent capture by enemy

"Killed her without hesitation, I mean you were a sleep killing machine." she held up her hand, expecting a high five. "Don't leave me hanging." Elizabeth looked at her hand for a moment before turning back to her computer, ticking the box at the bottom of the screen that showed that she found nothing suspicious about the death. "Do you even remember his name?"

"No," Elizabeth replied, seeing that Jane still hadn't lowered her arm. "I just remember that I got a medal for it, apparently he was a high ranked spy with Matulog." Jane finally lowered arm and disappeared around the divider separating their desk. Elizabeth resumed working

Name: Zoey Wllington
Gender: Female (she/her)
Age: 33
Address: 8 Heyfields Cottages, Tittensor Road, Tittensor",ST12 9HG
Cause of death: Incorrect opinion on the taste and cost of coffee
Note: cover face and name tag during transfer

"Got anything interesting?" Elizabeth asked, shouting over the divider.

"Someone very interesting." she replied, Elizabeth could hear the smile spread across her face.

"Who?" she asked.

"Danni Davis," Jane answered "Come and have a look." Elizabeth stood up and walked around the devideder , stopping to look at Jane's computer which did indeed bear the name of Danni Davis.

Name:Danni Davis
Gender: Female (she/her)
Age: 29
Address: 86 Ashton Road, Hyde",SK14 4RN

Cause of death: Matulog bomb she planted in a coffee shop.
Note: Member of Matulog

"So she's dead ?" Elizabeth asked, smiling softly to herself, right in Jane's face.

"Correct," Jane replied, smiling back "thought her betrayal would go unpunished then boom, shot right in the face, we might not have got her but we got her daughter and, Benny willing, we will get the son too." she held her eyes closed, crossing both fingers as Elizabeth wandered back to her desk, one more report had found her screen while she was away.

Name: Ramsha Rodriguez
Gender: Invalid Response "gender neutral they/them"
Age: 34
Address: Grey Walls, Crowlink Lane, Friston,BN20 0AX
Cause of death: unknown
Notes: Somnus Watches over us

This time she ticked a different box, one labelled "under suspicious circumstances"

"I got one." Elizabeth called out as she waited for the report to print, grabbing it fresh from the printer, holding it in the air, the A4 pages folding over her hand.

"One what?" Jane asked. Without speaking Elizabeth handed Jane the page, watching as her eyes scanned side to side, stopping wide on the notes section. "You got an unproductive," Jane leapt up, attempting to hug Elizabeth over the divider but instead hurt her chest against it, winding her. "Let's go." She stood back up and grabbed Elizabeth's wrist pulling her away from her desk, then stopping and turning back, grabbing her PCD and getting another cup, Elizabeth followed grabbing another for herself and followed Jane through the office to the machine at the front of the room just off to the side of the door. Janer placed her PCD in the machine anxiously waiting for the buzzing and the beeping to stop.

"Are you sure you wanna go?" Elizabeth asked, "I'm sure you'd rather be back at your desk." Elizabeth took the PCD out of the machine and replaced it with her own, handing the first back to Jane.

"Have you already forgotten what happened last time?" Jane replied as they both waited for the machine to fill up.

"No, I haven't forgotten but I think it's better if I go alone." Her PCD was nearly full.

"I didn't want to tell you this but." she hesitated, grabbing Elizabeth by the arm and pulling her to the side "Hariold told me keep an eye on you." Someone walked passed and Jane stopped talking, just laughing during which Elizabeth looked at her surroundings, four heads that could once be seen over the dividers were no longer there, and the clicking of the keys had become quieter, but imperceivably so. The beeping stopped . "Now get your PCD, we're leaving." Elizabeth continued looking back at the desks, the clicking of the keys has become even quieter as people stood up for their desks and dragged bodies for their desks a line forming at the window as one after another bodies were dropped into the barely stable pile, she thought about how she probably knew their employee numbers. A tear dropped from her eye which she wiped away with her sleeve

"Does it ever scare you?" Elizabeth asked when she saw Jane hold the door open.

"Does what?" Jane replied

"People are dying all around us. Jane followed through the door and pushed the button for the lift, waiting as the number above the door to reach the floor they're on. Floor two.

"What I think doesn't matter." she said repeatedly pressing the button "they have been as productive as they can be. Now all we can do is continue to rebuild." Floor five. The door opened before them and Jane stepped in. "I hope you're not letting that unproductive get to you." she said as she gestured for Elizabeth to stand next to her.

Cup of Sleep

Elizabeth followed pressing the button on the wall marked by a solitary capital G.

"Ground," Jane suddenly said at Elizabeth's said "ground floor, ground coffee, the grind. Do you know what they have in common?" Elizabeth simply shook her head "they are the foundation of our life. The ground we walk on, so we can run. The smell of a fresh cup waiting every quarter of an hour, my life blood. The reason we are alive and the path to recovery, work work work. That's why I am thankful for Benny."

Chapter Eleven
Sleep like death

Company policy sixteen: the RPCD (remote personal coffee device) is a small implant on the base of the brain that supplies the body with the recommended amount of caffeine. Experimental only, all tests prove fatal

Jane pressed her fingers against the wall and began to push her joints turning white with the force.

"What are you doing?" Elizabeth asked as she watched approaching slowly and grabbing her by the shoulder, turning her so they were standing face to face

"There's nothing in the way yet I can't seem to get through," she formed her hand into a fist and slammed it against the wall, pulling it back as she cut it on a sharp stone, blood pouring from the wound. Elizabeth saw the blood stain on the wall, walked up to Jane and grabbed her wrist,

"Stop it you idiot," she said, pulling her away from the wall. Yet she stopped mid sentence and looked back at the wall, Elizabeth heard the faint buzz again, words forming from the sound which hung in the back of her mind "the world is in ruin," it spoke "the world could be better," and one final phrase before returning to the first, its order unaltering "there is no room in the new world for the unproductive."

"What's wrong?" Jane asked after she finally freed her hand from Elizabeth's grasp, her other hand wrapped around the part that turned red with the pressure and force.

"Nothing." but then she paused, wanting to push her luck "Can't you hear that?" she asked, lifting her head and listening and the words became louder, her body shaking at the last one, the word unproductive.

"Hear what?" Jane asked, cupping her ear and listening to the silence. "Okay, we let ourselves get distracted," Jane said as she removed the PCD from her pocket and poured its contents directly into her mouth, prompting Elizabeth to do the same which she reluctantly did, seeing the brown liquid flow through her similarly shaded teeth as the smell overwhelmed her, to sugar or caramel only the pure caffeine which dried her throat. "What's his name?" Jane asked as she placed her device back in her pocket " Ramsha Rodrigez?" Elizabeth took the printed report from her pocket and read the details

"Ramsha Rodriguez" she answered "just a few minutes from here." They walked silently, Elizabeth's thoughts rushing through her head loudly until they reached the door frame, fragments of green wood hanging off the twisted and partly melted hinges.

Cup of Sleep

"Hello!" Jane yelled through the gap in the door as she leaned against it, cutting her hand on the sharp remains of the hinges. Elizabeth rushed over and took her by the wrist, rubbing her dust covered finger over the cut causing Jane to wince.

"That looks bad" Elizabeth remarked as the small amount of blood on her thumb rolled down and onto her arm eventually landing silently on the floor "I'll start the investigation while you go and find a plaster or something." Without complaint she took some Spunod from her pocket and ran from sight. Alone now Elizabeth entered the building not a moment too soon as the rain began pouring from the sky. "Ramsha," she called into the darkness of a room not even lit by the sun, for the curtains and blinds were closed. "I'm not here to hurt you." She saw the cracking and falling of the stone before she heard the bang as the bullet from the unseen firearm.

"Go away" they yelled from the door which led to the only lit room in the house "I'm dead." They fired again, Missing as Elizabeth ducked around the frame, out of view breathing deeply, her heartbeat audible like a drum in her head. Yet she tried to think of something to say, something to calm them down, a third short rang, punching through the wall just above her head, she jumped from her sitting position and walked out through the empty door frame hand above her head and three words on her lips, her eyes closed as tight as she could "Danni sent me." she heard the gun drop from their hands with a thud and approaching footsteps.

"That's impossible," They collapsed on their knees infront of Elizabeth, who finally got a good look at them. As their brown hands rested against the pants of their brown uniform, blue eyes looking into Elizabeth's "Danni is dead." Elizabeth fell to her knees, looking Ramsha in their eyes and said.

"I know you have no reason to trust me," she held their hand in hers and rubbed the space between thumb and finger with her thumb. "I wouldn't trust me in your position but believe me, the reports of her death have been greatly exaggerated." Elizabeth removed her PCD from pocket and pressed a small blue button on the side twice, a small vial containing a deep brown liquid sliding out of a slot in the side of the device and into her open palm "Drink this," she said as she twisted off the lid and handed it to Ramsha.

"Why?" They asked

"Because someone is coming and they are loyal to Benny". They took and unseal vial and placed it against their lips, hesitating just before the first drop could pass

"What's this?" they asked

"Byritherol" Elizabeth explained "You drink it and then let go, I will take you to Danni but as I said you have to trust me, they think you're dead so getting you out of here will be easier." they looked up at Elizabeth, their eyes locking and with one final sentence they downed it all in a single gulp

"Searching for somnus." There was a moment after the liquid was gone that nothing happened, a brief moment of panic took Elizabeth as she thought her barely thought through plan had failed, then she saw their hand raising, grasping around the heart stiffly before stopping , falling to the floor with a painful sounding slam. It took five minutes for Jane to arrive, a large plasted over the cut on her hand and five more sticking out of her pocket.

"Is this him?" Jane asked, picking them up by the arms and gesturing for her to grab their legs.

"Yes, this is them." Elizabeth confirmed grabbing their ankles and lifting, first stumbling and dropping one of their legs but then supporting it with her knee "I got them." lowering their legs to the ground and moving Jane out of the way and lifting Ramsha's arm around the back her neck balancing them by wrapping her arm around their waist

"You sure?" Jane asked, wiping something off her arms and then her legs.

"Yeah," Elizabeth replied, "someone needs to go back and finish the follow-up paperwork." The plaster on her hand had already become a deep shade of crimson as

111111Andrew James King

she removed the pleaser and replaced it with one her pocket, "plus that's probably gonna need stitches," the old plaster fell to the floor, landing on one of the carpets and sticking to it.

"You're probably right." she sighed "Just make sure you get him back on time."

"Don't worry." Elizabeth Replied "they'll go where they need to." They both wandered off, parting ways at the door and wishing each other luck as Elizabeth struggled with the body.

$$_{z}zZ$$

It took half an hour for Elizabeth to make it back to the safehouse, stumbling and falling over Ramsha legs as they waved side to side in the air, their boots slamming into her ankle until she found the door William waiting on one side and Danni on the other rushing to catch Ramsha and Elizabeth as they both fell to the floor

"Are they okay?" Danni asked carrying Ramsha into the house, through door after door and into the room in which the sleep pod stood, surrounded by darkness lit by a mix of red, green and yellow lights which meant it was in use but nearly finished

Cup of Sleep

"Yeah, they're fine." Elizabeth confirmed as she watched the door slide open and a body rest, kept till by sitips of velcro and fabric which wrapped around the wrist, ancle, neck and stomach, but it was not Charlie.

"Oh, before she fully wakes up I think I should tell you who this is. This is Evie-May Schaefer" she awoke and as soon as she was ready to stand the straps were removed and in her place they put Ramsha, the pod activating as soon as the pod was sealed.

"How did you trick her?" Danni asked as she fell to the ground, covered in sweat and dirt "Couldn't have been easy to trick someone as loyal as Jane."

"She's back at the office, getting stitches for a cut in her hand and writing the paperwork confirming Ramsha is dead, they expect a body though."

"Just say you were attacked and the body was stolen." she suggested

"Stolen by who?" Elizabeth asked

"Me" she answered

"It won't work." Elizabeth replied

"Why?" Danni asked

"They think you're dead. Jane showed me the paperwork, they all think you died in the coffee shop explosion, a suicide bomb."

"Ramsha?" She asked "they were there at the time."

"But people think they're dead." Elizabeth countered. A third person joined in, weakly stumbling towards the pair before clumsily falling into a nearby chair

"I could do it." Evie-may suggested

"No," Danni commanded. "We're trying to fake your death, we don't want any extra attention on your name."

"Maybe she killed me" she said, pointing to Elizabeth "as I took the body she stabbed me with a shard of glass or something."

"They will want to question me again, probably a medical examination." she gave a small nod of approval, watching as everyone filtered out of the room Elizabeth grabbing hold of William's wrist just before he left

"I need to talk to you." Elizabeth said as she pulled him back into the room.

"The morgue is just a few levels below the infirmary." was all she said, looking as his face went from confused to understanding before sticking to refusal

"No, you can't!" he yelled, louder than he intended for he moved closer and whispered "I don't think they'd leave a place like that unguarded and even if they did how are you gonna get the body out of there?" she didn't have an answer

Cup of Sleep

"Please help me." she begged "I owe her that much." William grabbed Elizabeth by both shoulders, slightly bending his knees so they stood eye to eye

"You did not kill Sarah," he explained "the police officer who shot her did. Trust me, Danni doesn't blame you."

"But I do," Elizabeth replied, "How do you think the police knew?" She asked.

"I don't know but if what Danni told me is right it was one of your co-workers, Jane." He explained

"And how do you think Jane found out?" William didn't answer, instead he pulled up two chairs and placed them facing one another, both sat.

"She blames herself." he told her "Thinks that if she had been a better mother both her children would still be alive. Sarah, still alive and Charlie." he paused "Charlie isn't doing well."

"I haven't seen him since we left the factory, it feels like so long ago." Elizabeth felt her eyes closing, fighting against it but feeling herself slip.

"You don't need to worry about that." William said smiling "this is a safe place to sleep." with every second the struggle became harder and harder "good night." She drifted off, her sleep marked by flashes of light and originless noise before calm and stillness, that night she did not dream. She woke up beneath the blanket of a bed with no recollection of how she got there, just sound of the voice in her ear, reminding her of the ruined world she once saw.

"Did you know you snore?" William asked, seeing that she had woken up "like a pig." He laughed as he helped her out of bed and onto her feet.

"I what?" she asked, her vision clearing slowly

"Oh, yeah I forgot. No sleep." his laughing stopped "I'll explain what snoring is later but for now we need to get you back to work. You have a room to map and a body to recover, Somnus be with you." He left the room, placing a pair of casual working clothes on the end of the bed and waiting for her to get dressed.

Chapter Twelve
carpe diem

Company policy seventy five: one spunod is equal to the average cost of a cup of coffee in your area

This morning the wind was bitter cold, Elizabeth and William were using the collar of their uniform to protect what little of their face they could as the dust and the leaves blew through the air

"Thousands of people have died." William said as they rounded the corner, passing the park, facing the monolithic office building. Darkened by the all encompassing shadow of Benny, whose neatly polished face and newly repainted eyes watched over both of them as they walked from one side of the street to the other.

"Correct," Elizabeth confirmed "their bodies are piled next to the front door of the office. What's your idea?" They were standing in a heavily shaded side of the building beneath an unpopulated balcony.

"Well, when the plan of faking deaths first formed we got the blueprints to this building, our plan was to put someone in and wait till they were trained but since we have you we don't need to do that. I found on those blueprints a chute attached to the side and ending here. We should find out where it goes." he reched into his pocket and pulled out a torch shining it into the darkness, taking a moment to find and then highlight a metallic hole in the wall above a metal bin

"You think it gets into the morgue?" Elizabeth asked as she approached the bin, using it to climb up to the chute but falling backwards as they were overwhelmed by the smell of rot and decay. William grabbed her by the shoulders before she could hit the floor, slowly lowering her to the ground.

"I present." he said using his other hand to gesture towards the bin "the bodies of the unproductive."

"Do you think she's in there?" Elizabeth asked as she slowly approached the bin.

"No," he said "they're probably trying to think of some justifican for killing a child, planting evidence on her body. People are willing to accept a lot in the name of productivity but not the death of a child that looks like their own." They slowly lowered the lid, holding their breath as the sudden gust of wind blew the smell and flies towards their uncovered faces. "Ladies first." he said cupping his hands beneath his knees forming a step.

"Why me?" Elizabeth asked, he spoke under his breath so she didn't hear, "What was that?" she asked

"Because I'm too big to fit through the chute." she saw his shoulders lower when he finished speaking but he didn't say anything else, he just waited as she rested one foot on his hands. using both of her hands to balance pulled herself onto the lid and on level with the chute its, smooth metallic surface barely big enough for her to fit through. "Wear this." he said as he handed her a mask, a gas mask like the one she wore in the factory. "They can take it off," he explained "but if you're faster than them they won't know who you are." his voice became deeper, his expression tightening "that is of utmost importance." the moment the mask covered her face she could hear her own breath, feel the leather tight against her face.

"Wish me luck." Elizabeth said as she grabbed the sides of the chute and pulled herself though not waiting for a reply. She moved through the chute showly, each of her movements echoing through the long narrow tunnel low enough to climb but steep enough to cause difficulty. she pulled herself through the chute, hearing from the other side of the tunnel a conversation that made her pause and press her ear against the cold metal.

"Are you sure it's gonna work?" a muffled voice said "she is a child." the loud sound of hand hitting face rang through the room and into the tunnel as a less muffled voice yelled

"She's an unproductive! Daughter of a Matulog member, a very high up one if I hear correctly!"

"A dead member," the first person corrected "killed by her own bomb, blowing up a coffee shop,"

"Are you sure she's dead?" the second person asked

"Of course she is, it was all over the news." the first person explained "or do you believe what Harold has been saying."

"Just shut up and bring the body, we need to frame her for something." The second person dismissed. Elizabeth found a gap in the chute through which she could hear the conversation, a man and woman spoke over a pale corpse, one that had not long ago asked where her father was.

"Do you remember who she kidnapped?" The woman asked "Elizabeth something?"

"Elizabeth Clair. Why?" The man asked

"What if she killed Elizabeth somehow?"

"That won't work, everyone knows she is still alive." He explained

"For now, but you've read the report, they forced her into a sleep pod, they could have done anything to her while she was asleep." Elizabeth clasped her hands over her mouth silencing a scream.

"Are you suggesting we break her coffee machine?" she asked

120120Andrew James King

Cup of Sleep

"No," He countered, "something inside." a smile spread across his face

"The overdose chip?" she asked. Elizabeth didn't stay to hear any more of the conversation , backing out of the vent so careless about where her knees landed that she overstepped the opening of the chute and fell down, landing on her back and rolling off, catching herself on the ground with her hands, her nose an inch off the ground.

"Elizabeth!" William yelled as he grabbed underneath her shoulders and lifted her up, turning her so she could rest against the bin.

"She's in there," Elizabeth explained, her breath laboured and forced, her hand on her chest.

"Slow down," William said "Were you seen?" He asked

"No" Elizabeth replied

"Then why the rush?" he sat on the stoney ground in front of her inspecting her arms for cuts

"They're gonna kill me."

"Who?" William asked, wrapping his arm under her shoulders and helping her to her feet.

"The company." she explained "They're gonna say Sarah had something to do with it." They began walking, not towards the safehouse, but around the building one turn away from the front door.

Cup of Sleep

"There's something I need you to do." William said as they stopped walking "you have been absent for too long, people are gonna start getting suspicious." Elizabeth pushed open the glass door by its handles, passed into the barely maintained reception area and approached the desk behind which a woman slept. Elizabeth pressed the button of the bell. Nothing. She pushed it again, harder this time and leaned over the desk and whispered to the sleeping woman.

"Wake up." she pressed it again six times in rapid succession till she heard a door open. She ran into the waiting area, leaping over the corner sofa and looked up over it. Three security guards entered through the door, dark aprons over their front.

"looks like someone's tired." one of them mocked her as he picked up the bell and threw it at her head, the ring sound mixed with the blunt force causing her to fall backwards off her chair and hit her head against the ground. She woke up, looking up at the guards around her and panicked, then she heard a beep, a low almost imperceptible beep from her desk. Her nose bled and then she was on the ground once more. Unmoving, not even the slow rise and fall of her chest to show life. They grabbed her underneath her elbow, one person per side, and pulled her away from the desk, her legs and hands knocking against tables, walls and chairs with quick carelessness.

122122Andrew James King

Cup of Sleep

One stayed behind, lifting up the eye covering of his helmet and locking eyes with the spot in front of the door. Muddy footsteps marked the entrance as well as a small trail of blood which stopped just before the desk and turned to the waiting area, over the couch. Elizabeth scanned her body and saw a small cut on the back of arm just above her elbow, she placed her hand over it, wandering when she had gotten it and then as the guard approached the door walking quickly passed the reception, picking up a paper towel from the janitor's closet and entering the lift holding the towel to the cut. The lift rose slowly, the music from the half broken speaker barely audible. Then the door opened, her place being taken by two other people as Elizabeth stepped onto more stable ground and into the office where everyone was typing with deafening clicks as they wrote the information of every death, every heart attack as around them the same thing was happening to their co workers, their bodies dragged along the rough carpeted floor and thrown on the pile before resuming work.

"Good morning." Elizabeth said as she slipped through the crowded cubicles and around the people carrying more paperwork than they could safely carry. Yet more people dropped dead, the paper falling to the ground and darkening as it landed on spilled coffee only to be

123Andrew James King

picked up by passing workers who just added it to the top of their pile.

"Good morning Elizabeth." Jane said as Elizabeth found her desk and logged on to her computer, quickly working through her work for the day

Name: Alexander Powell
Gender: Male
Age: 23
address: 47 Angerton Avenue, Shiremoor ,NE27 0TU
Cause of death: PCD broken in shootout
Notes: Must investigate possible connection to stolen sleep pod

This death she accepted, passing it forward to the general pile and moving on, either accepting the deaths or marking them for investigation. "Drink." Jane said handing Elizabeth her PCD "Don't wanna be one of those unproductives. She made herself a cup of coffee, the taste she remembered loving so much now causing her face to crease with such intensity, so much as she could not drink it all at once, instead placing the cup on her desk and stopping to take small sips throughout the next few hours

Name: Jamie Rawson
Gender: male

Age: 20
address: 71 Barry Avenue, Stoke-On-Trent",ST2 8AE
Cause of death: non-coffee related heart attack
Notes: no previous record of his existence

Another death that Elizabeth passed on, filling out the other details and clicking accept.

"Did you get that guy back?" Jane asked looking over the wall of her cubicle "the one we got from his house."

"Yes," Elizabeth answered, "I got them back. They're in the morgue." Another death appeared on her screen, one that made her pause and wait, rubbing her eyes, checking, hoping she was dreaming, but she wasn't.

Name: Elizabeth Claire
Gender: Female
Age: 28
address: "169 Edge Lane, Edge Hill",L7 2PF
Cause of death: Slow acting poison injected by child of Matulog agent
Notes: Death has already been investigated.

She rejected this death, clicking on the button and writing "still alive" in the pop up box that appeared "That's weird." she said louder than she intended as Jane rested her hand against the back of Elizabeth's chair and looked at her screen

"What's weird?" she asked, taking the mouse and looking through the case history.

"It says I died." Elizabeth replied

"To be fair," she answered, "you were missing for a while, and a lot of people just assumed you were dead. It probably just took a while for this one to come through, glitch in the system."

"Then why is there a cause of death? Shouldn't it just say something like missing or unknown?" it seems very specific." Jane clicked the back arrow and closed her death page

"It doesn't matter." she told Elizabeth "you've said it was a mistake and that is it. Just get back to work and finish your coffee. It's getting cold." Jane stood there, arms folded as Elizabeth turned back to her computer and went back to work. "Did you not hear what I said?" Jane picked up the cup of cold coffee and with one hand turned the chair around so they were facing each other and with one hand forced her mouth open, pouring the coffee down her throat giving her no chance to breathe. She swallowed most of it, choking on the rest and leaning on her knees trying to catch her breath, breathing deeply in and out.

"What was that for?" Elizabeth asked using a nearby tissue to wipe the coffee off the side of her mouth

Cup of Sleep

"You weren't drinking your coffee." she answered "I couldn't allow that.

127Andrew James King

Chapter Thirteen
Unlucky

Company policy twenty nine: all suspected spies are to be reported to your immediate superior.

A week had passed yet nothing had happened, Elizabeth sat at her desk typing away at an hour unknown to her as all the clocks ticked at a different rate and the hours she did know merged into one. It had been a while since Elizabeth had received any resorts so she was in her cubicle looking over the walls to Jane's computer, watching her accept and reject reports one after another when one came up, in the brief moment when she blinked a report appeared on her screen.

Name: Aleena Freeman
Gender: Female
Age: 32
Address: "22 St Davids Avenue, Dover",CT17 9HU
Cause of death: coffee machine made toilet juice instead of coffee
Notes: possible Matulog agent on route

Cup of Sleep

"Jane." Elizabeth said catching her attention before her eyes could drift back to the computer. Elizabeth walked around the short barrier and grabbing the back of Jane's chair, turning it around so she was facing with her back to the screen with no chance of seeing out of her peripheral vision. "This case looks interesting," Elizabeth leaned over and scanned the address, trying to get it into her head before she clicked accept, her other hand of Jane's head doing what she could to stop her from turning her head

Name: Jane Ender
Gender: Female
Age: 19
Address: Wolds View, 1 Glebe Garth, Wetwang",YO25 9BP
Cause of death: Unrelated heart attack
Notes: nothing of interest

Eventually Elizabeth let got of Jane's head letter her turn her chair around and look back at the screen taking a moment to read the report that had just come through before turning her head back to Elizabeth and asking

"I don't see anything interesting?" before dismissing the report

"She has the same name as you." Elizabeth pointed out pulling the record back up and pointing to the name. "Drink." she said taking Jane's PCD and pouring a cup out then reaching over and doing the same with hers downing the full cup and coughing as she could barely hold down the contents, burning her tongue and cheeks as the liquid caused her eyes to tear up.

"Thank you." Jane said as she downed her drink, the hot liquid spilling on her chin. she went back to work, Elizabeth walked away, passed her desk and towards the door pushing it, almost getting through before a hand grasped her shoulder with force and stopped her.

"Harold?" Elizabeth asked "good morning sir" the coffee still stained his breath as he spoke through his dry lips and dark teeth.

"Meet me in my office, Miss. Clair." He walked away quickly, pushing past people and rolling the dead ones to the side with his foot in a way so casual it looked to be part of his walk . Elizabeth followed, helping those who had fallen off the floor and placing their documents on nearby tables and trying her best to keep up with her boss who shrank more and more into the distance before disappearing behind set of doors that swung back and forth with the force of his push. She waited for the doors to stop and then pushing them open herself, his thunderous footsteps showing her where she needed to go without following the signs. She turned corner after corner stopping at the door, ignoring his assistant as she pushed it with her full shoulder and entered the now messy office the only part of it untouched being two leather chairs that faced each other on opposite sides of what she assumed was once a desk but now looked like a pile of splinters scattered to the wind.

"Sorry about the mess." he said as he sat on his chair and gestured for Elizabeth to do the same "though I'd be surprised if a bit of mess was enough to bother you after everything you have been through." The compartment in which his predecessor had hidden the sleep pod wide open, the back wall full of holes, the pointed edges covered in blood which drew her attention to the long cuts of Harold's hand, going from nail to knuckle long and deep barely healed with the occasional drop leaking through and staining the ground at his feet and the shoes he wore.

"I'm sorry sir I don't think I understand?" She replied, taking her seat and pushing the remains of the desk out of the way.

"Do you know anything about Norse mythology?" he asked in response to Elizabeth's question.

"Just the traitor goddess Nótt, of the night." He opened two of the windows though the air outside seemed still, making the room no warmer or colder. "How about Huginn and Muninn" Two ravens landed on the ledge of the windows that just pecked the plastic which held the glass in place. Harold placed his hand at and their talons which bloodlessly clutched his fingers as he picked them up and brought them closer to Elizabeth.

"Huginn and Muninn, better known as thought and memory, would fly all over midgard telling their master Odin. and like their master they exchanged their eye for that knowledge." Elizabeth looked deep into one of the void-like eyes of the birds and saw her own reflection upon its lens-like eye. The birds resting on her shoulders their beaks a few centimetres away from her eye.

"I have seen everything." Harold said as he picked the leg of the desk off the ground and resisted it on his shoulder and over the back of his neck. Elizabeth got off her chair and walked back to the door, not taking her eyes of the towering figure who swung the wooden plank over her head as she ducked underneath and dashed forward using all her might to push him away but failing, falling to the ground as though she had attempted to push a brick wall he reached into the rubble and pushed a button, a quiet slam sounded from the door and when Elizabeth tried to push it open the door would not budge.

"Twice you have disappeared, twice you have come back with barely a scratch on you despite being seen in the company of treacherous sleepers and the silly theys and thems." he threw the plank to the side and lunged forward with he hands, grasping Elizabeth by her shoulders and lifting her off the ground so that he and she were eye level and wordlessly he threw her to the ground, her hand feeling the tiny pricks of a dozen splinters and one long cut along her arm as she slammed into the desk, she reached over for a plank and raised it.

"This is not what it looks like." she said as she held it before her defensively the beam blocked her vision of his face so only his arms and legs were visible. She swung, the heavy wood clashing with his skull and sending him falling backwards towards his desk, catching himself and rolling to avoid landing on the splinters. Elizabeth swung again, landing on his ribs with a deafening crack and throwing it to the side leaning against the door. He wasn't getting up but his chest still rose and fell with a calming consistency as she calmed down. The beating of her heart slowed, with every passing second the pain in her arm became more apparent, a dull pushing pain that was getting worse by the second. She searched his office, pulling drawers from the desk and opening cupboard till she found a first aid kit wrapping the bandage around her arm and holding it in place with some tape she found beneath a crack in the wall. She rolled her sleeve down to cover it, waiting as the amount of blood dripping from the cut stopped. She found the button in the rubble and pushed it, unlocking the door and leaving Harold's receptionist sitting on the floor behind her desk head tucked between her knees. Running past her, through the hallways and crashing into the main office, everyone seeming ignorant of what had just happened, typing away at their computers. She ran past them, ignoring the eyes which just now rose up and watched her as she sprintered to where she knew the morgue was. She walked despite knowing she was being watched, first the curious onlookers who knew she wasn't supposed to be there but didn't care to the cameras which seemed to rotate on the wall to track her every step. Elizabeth pushed open the heavy wooden doors and saw the coffee stained room which held the bodies of both the productive and the unproductive, the productive held in private space while the unproductive were piled in the corner of the room left to rot as some of them had started to do the smell so intense she had to hold her breath to approach the pile and start rooting through it, the tags tied to their feet carrying not names but numbers, twenty five, forty seven, sixty eight and then the body she was looking for one hundred and seventy two, Sarah Davis. Elizabeth grabbed the body by the wrist, slowly pulling it from the others and cradled it in her arms, the lifeless pale eyes staring into hers as she breathed deeply, fighting back tears.

"Let's get you back to your mother." she said using her thumb to close both of Sarah's eyes. She ran towards the escape chute but found it shut and locked, voices echoed from somewhere Elizabeth could not find.

"Where are you going with that body Elizabeth?" they said, a female voice. Elizabeth ran, using her foot to open the door and holding it open with her back, doing her best to make sure nothing touched the body she was carrying. "Who did you think you were tricking?" the same voice asked again and again Elizabeth ignored it as she ran through the halls which seemed longer than before, their walls blending into one another like a maze. "Where is the sleep pod? With the child?" The lights in the attached room flicked on and off quickly.

"You stay away from him!" Elizabeth yelled as she watched the lights turn on and saw Jane on the other side of the glass.

"Struck a nerve, have I?" she laughed as she walked back through the way she came, Elizabeth running towards the main office, using her back to slowly open the door, seeing the large screen at the end of the room, Harold's face large on its many monitors

"Elizabeth Claire is a traitor, <one hundred> spunod to the first person that catches her." The door was locked, she was surrounded, she made her way to the back of the room and opened the window. Looking deep into the eyes of the Benny Beans mascot. Eyes that saw all, heard all, knew all. They saw as the former employee of cubicle C27 of the heart attack division of the incident report room felt for the lock that kept the window shut. She turned to face her co-workers, chairs and keyboards in hand, murder in their eyes. Without looking Elizabeth pushed the window open and spoke to her enraged co-worker.

"Do you remember the first time you saw Benny?" she gestured to the statue with her head but no one responded "most would be inspired, some would run. But not I," she stepped backwards, the heel of her shoe hanging on empty air "When I looked into the eyes of Benny I saw a powerful force, one that could shape a nation with its size and addiction. And I decided no more." She closed her eyes, her only assurance that she was not alone being the yells of those around her which got louder and louder with each breath she took, she took one final step back and felt the ground beneath her feet no more. She was falling, the air rushing past her head and through her hair as, sooner than she expected, she felt the force against her back and came to a rest, her mind overwhelmed by the darkness than followed, her fear over what happened to Sarah replace by an unknown euphoria as her vision faded into darkness. The darkness was breached by a light, a voice which called for her in the distance, a woman sitting on a park bench wearing a suit patting the seat next to her. Slowly Elizabeth made her way over to the bench and sat, taking a moment to embrace the silence. She could not feel the breeze around her, nor hear the bird chirp as they rose up with the quickly rising sun.

"Hello Elizabeth." the woman said as she stood up and sat on the back of the beach

"Hello Somnus." Elizabeth replied "I must be dreaming." Somnus didn't say anything. She just laughed.

Chapter Fourteen
Crash

Company policy four hundred: any mention of any gods/powerful beings involved in the history of sleep will be grounds for imprisonment unless in the context of slander.

"Walk with me." was the first thing she said after a moment of quiet, as the sound of the birds came through and was all that could be heard as they sailed the light of the sun in the early morning of a day she knew not the day, month or year of.

"Where are we going?" Elizabeth asked standing up despite this lack of knowledge and following the god to the centre of the park. There stood a water fountain the edge of which was marked by symbols of different gods. The fountain itself a statue of an average sized man wearing a robe which covered only his lower hand, a snake coiling up his staff. Asclepius, the word warped beneath the water of the fountain.

"You will know where you are when you wake up, if you wake up but for now I need to finish telling you the story." She cupped some of the water in the fountain in her hands and drank some of it, the pennys too large for the gap her lips made so fell at her feet. "Now drink." In spite of everything telling her not to, Elizabeth did as she was told, reaching into the fountain and taking a handful of the water out, tasting it for maybe the first time in her life. The water quenched a thirst so deep she didn't realise she felt it until the moment the cooling liquid entered her throat causing her to cough.

"What story?" Elizabeth leaned down and drank more water, even though in her mind she could not shake the phrase toilet juice.

"The one The Glass Lady wouldn't tell you." with a wave of her hand the silent scene before them melted away, falling like paint yet to dry revealing the roar of a battlefield. The building in disrepair, plains in the sky where there once was birds and tanks on the street where people once walked to work or the pub. "Follow them." she pointed to a man in a suit, briefcase by his side and the walking of a child, each step the small jump of someone with more energy than could be released. As they got closer they could hear what he was whispering, so silent that no one around him could hear.

> "We prepare our brew
> For the very tired few
> Sugar packs we pour
> Never more than four

Cup of Sleep

For Benny do we live
For Benny, do we Drink."

"Who's that?" Elizabeth asked, watching the man as he removed what had the appearance of a PCD from his pocket. It was bigger, with steam vents on the top and bottom and a screen which read "full capacity, two cups."

"A man whose name is irrelevant for now but whos title will change the world forever, but not in a good way." he stopped walking at the base of a stage and took a deep breath before ascending the three wooden steps and again resting behind a podium on which a single piece of paper sat and a pen, the pen was picked up and the paper signed. Then there was silence, even the bombs and the tanks they left behind them, that had before been almost deafening, went quiet. It didn't last long, soon a roar of cheers and clapping erupted in the crowd as with each of Elizabeth's blinks they changed, people, who previously wore casual clothes now robed in black body armour and aprons that hung loosely around their necks and over their torsos.

"What did he just sign?" Somnus just chuckled to herself, casually moving out of the way as the crowd charged passed them, knocking on the door and waiting for a response.

Cup of Sleep

"He has just murdered sleep," was all she said "the innocent sleep. Sore labour's bath." the people standing at the doors became more and more impatient, then the knocking stopped replaced by a thud, quickening in pace and fist was swapped for foot and then a hammer swung with enough force to knock the door off its hinges and after a few minutes people were dragged from their beds in various stages of decency, some confused, grasping onto their children who slipped further and further away as they were separated and some angry struggling against the uncountable amount of hands that struggled to keep them still. Somnus waved her hand and the world around them melted again in place of the fighting, bodies lay; children mourning over corpses whose faces could not be recognised. Elizabeth ran through the field of corpses, stepping over and round limbs towards one near the back, the child being one she recognised.

"Mom." she said to the child whose tear stained face rose up from the back from a grey haired old woman who lay face down on the concrete.The girl looked at Elizabeth, a confused look spreading across her face that was again overtaken by grief.

"She can't see you." Somnus explained placing her hand on Elizabeth's shoulder "not really." The pair stood up and for a moment waited in the silence.

Cup of Sleep

"My mom never told me how grandma died."
those few words breaking the silence as the scene around
them rushed to life, bodies abandoned on the street as
children were taken away leaving just the human and the
God in the middle of the street, the human lowered into the
god's embrace by her gentle arms and her soft shoulder to
cry on, to drift off into a peaceful sleep.

zZZ

Before her eyes opened she could hear the speaker, it's
loud voice blaring over the silence, describing her.
"Dark skin, blue eyes, black hair, five foot seven. The
unproductive is at large, any information leading to her
arrest will be rewarded." the message repeated over and
over again.

"She's awake." William said, his hand resting on
the back of Elizabeth's head holding it up slightly, as her
eyes opened and her vision cleared, she saw Danni,
Sarah's body in her hand cradling her, not looking up but
Elizabeth could tell from the sounds she was making, her
deep laboured breathing, Danni was crying.

"Danni," Elizabeth said, her voice a near silent
croak as Elizabeth placed her hand against the stony
ground and stood at full height, the world taking a moment
to stop spinning around her. She checked her bandages and

saw they were still white, the fabric unstained by blood or mud. She removed the bandage and in place of the long bleeding cut she expected to find was just one long, white scar. Elizabeth grabbed William by his arm and helped him up "He knows." was all she could say as she breathed deeply in and out.

"Who knows what?" Danni asked as she stood up, Sarah still in hands so full she could not wipe away the tears that fell, blocking her sight. Elizabeth approached and wiped them herself.

"Harold, he's known about me the whole time," again she saw the ravens circling above. "Get away from here!" Elizabeth yelled as she threw a stone at the watching fowl, missing.

"What's wrong?" the birds remained as William asked

"Those birds, they're not real birds. They're cameras. That's how he found out." William grabbed her wrist and dragged, slowly at first leading her and Danni though the street, towards the house, running though other abandoned houses though the front door and out the back looping till they looked up and saw the ravens circling another house, they stopped at the door of the safe house and rested, falling the ground to catch their breath.

"I'll get the shovel." William said, sliding the key out of his pocket and opening the door.

"What does he need a shovel for?" Danni asked

"We're going to the park to bury Sarah, with her father." Elizabeth explained

"But we didn't bury Alen, he's in the pile next to your office building." A few minutes later William emerged from the house, Charlie not far behind, he hands in his pockets until he saw Sarah

"Is she sleeping?" Charlie asked as Elizabeth took his hand and led him away from the group, sitting on one of the steps outside of the door so she could look him in the eye while looking forward.

"We're going to go see your dad okay." she said, brushing his hair out of his eyes "but after you won't be able to see him again." he lowered his head, a small tear streaming down his face.

"Is daddy dead?" he asked as Elizabeth stood up she didn't say anything in response but she couldn't tell she didn't have to.

"Let's go Charlie." Danni said, holding her hand out following behind William who carried both the body and the shovel leading them to the park, stopping at the head of the patch of dirt not yet covered in dirt he planted the shovel in the ground a few feet to the right and started digging. "When did you do this?" Danni asked as she took a seat on one of the benches, "bury Alen."

Cup of Sleep

"On our way back to get the sleep pod, I took his body from the pile and William grabbed a shovel, we buried him here but wanted to wait to get Sarah before we told you." Danni dived forward, wrapping her arms around Elizabeth and crying into her shoulder. "N is for noble, with a heart and soul which should be global," Elizabeth said as she chuckled to herself.

"What did you say?" Danni asked looking up, her eyes marked with a pale red.

"Nothing." Elizabeth replied "just remembering something William told me."

"He told you about the poem?" she asked

"Yeah, while we were burying Alen we were talking about how we knew him. I thought it was funny." Danni started chuckling herself

"I thought it was romantic." she answered

"I'm not saying it wasn't but some of the things he said. So unlike the man I met." Elizabeth explained

"That is because he is on the job, in a hostile environment, when he's back at the base he is a completely different man."

"Wanna take over?" William asked, holding the shovel over his head.

"Of course loverboy." the pair laughed

"What?" he asked

"Nothing." Elizabeth said as he approached and took the shovel out of his hand and watched as he walked over to Danni, taking the place on the bench Elizabeth once sat on. Picking up the shovel she began digging, looking around her, seeing Charlie standing by himself, throwing a ball he had found against the wall with one hand and catching it with the other he spoke but she could not see who to, if anyone. She did not focus on digging but her arms moved anyway, throwing the dirt to her side on the pile that William had formed with his digging, Elizabeth dag, lifting piles of dirt from the ground and tossing them to the side until finally she saw William approach and grab her hand.

"I think that's enough." he said as he slowly took the shovel. *He's right* Elizabeth thought as she fell to the ground beside the hole her forehead drenched in sweat. As William brought the body over Elizabeth watched as he, with such care and attention lowered the body into the hole and went back to retrieve the shovel.

"Did he ever talk about me?" Danni asked as she stood over the patch of ground under which her husband lay "I know he probably didn't but I just want to know for sure."

"He spoke about you and the kids occasionally," Elizabeth answered "like when we bumped into each other refilling our PCDs but not very often." Danni gave a silent nod as she removed her wedding band and paced it on the ground, using her hand to scoop up some of the surrounding dirt and covering it.

"We should go." Danni said standing up and facing the exit to the park.

"Do you and Charlie want some time alone to be with them?" William asked. At the mention of his name Charlie stopped focusing on the ball, letting it fly past his head as he made his way towards his mother and grabbed her hand.

"I'm honestly glad you made this possible," she explained, "but I think we need to get out of here. There's just too many people they are looking for in one place for them to not be looking for us."

"Where are we going?" Elizabeth asked as Danni started making her way out of the park

"We need to get another communicator, send a message to Matulog. Let them know our rescue is urgent."

Chapter Fifteen
The Message

Company policy three hundred seventy nine: Any attempt to contact forces outside the bounds of company grounds will be considered reason for termination and banishment without coffee.

They went back to the base and one at a time used the sleep pod, preparing for the mission to come. First Charlie whose hour in the pod was fitful, his eyes still marked with tears which rolled down his face and onto the floor of the pod, then William who seemed almost peaceful in his sleep, a small smile spreading across his face as he lay there unmoving. Then it was Danni whose sleep seemed to be a mix of the two before, still in her place like William but tears could still be seen pouring down her face through the glass lid of the pod. Finally Elizabeth slept, unaware of how she slept just of the calming words in her head that soothed her busy mind into silence, not a thought of betrayal, murder or blood crossing her mind as what should have been eight hours of sleep passed in one.

"You ready?" Danni asked, knocking on the glass after her hour was done.

Cup of Sleep

"Aren't the other two coming with us?" Elizabeth asked as the straps were undone and she dropped to the floor

"Ramshin is," Danni explained "they used to work where we are going but Evie isn't, we need someone to stay here and guard the pod. Hide it in case we have any visitors." After getting new clothes, the pair met William and Ramshin in the front room of the house.

"Why are we leaving now?" Ramshin asked, "There are still agents in the field."

"Too many of us have been compromised." Danni explained "the longer we are here the more likely we are to get caught." Danni rached into a bag and removed four masks, featureless except small speakers sticking out of the forehead.

"What are these for?" Elizabeth asked as the flipped the switch on top of the speaker, a voice saying on repeat

"You are alone." in a low boring voice.

"Do you hear the speakers?" Danni asked. Elizabeth turned off the speaker and held her breath, listening to the air around her.

"The world is in ruin," it spoke "the world could be better," and one final phrase before returning to the first, its order unaltering "there is no room in the new

149Andrew James King

world for the unproductive." the speakers said loud enough to be heard from anywhere.

"And people believe it." Danni explained "the coffee has made them suggestible, they see whatever the speakers tell them to. They see what these speakers tell them they do."

"Why don't you use them all the time?" Elizabeth asked

"Because it doesn't just make us disappear, it makes everyone around them disappear. They become completely alone. That would look suspicious. To be in a room full of people and then to be alone." She placed the mask over her face and handed them out to the other two who both did the same, Elizabeth being the last to put hers on.

"Where are we going?" Elizabeth asked, her breath trapped in the mask, a horrid smell.

"The police station." William answered "when someone needs to take out a communication device they need to go to the police, file a report. Which means they are probably kept there. We are going to steal one of them and go back to the cinnamon factory, send the more urgent message." he turned to face Danni "spelling the name right this time." he laughed and a few seconds later Danni joined in.

Cup of Sleep

"It's not an easy word to spell." Danni explained as she removed her mask and checked the speaker, turning it on to listen to it speak once and then putting it back on. "Now let's go." All four left the house one after another, Danni first then Elizabeth followed by Willam and finally Ramsha. They walked through the street, through abandoned buildings and small shops until they had no choice but to be in public, walking past the building Elizabeth used to work in, seeing the impact her fall had on the pile of bodies, remains scattered on the ground with people either stepping around them, pushing them out the way with sticks or just walking over them, high heels and muddy work boots on exposed backs digging into shoulder blades.

"Do you think Alex will send people to collect us?" Ramsha asked.

"She has to," William replied, "we are some of her best agents."

"But we have someone they haven't met." they replied "we don't know if they will trust this Elizabeth."

"You trusted me." Elizabeth countered

"Because I had to." Ramsha answered "It was trust you or die."

"And do you regret trusting me?" Elizabeth asked

" No." they replied they made the rest of the walk in silent, not removing the masks but not turning the speakers on ignoring the looks they got as they walked through the street and stopped in front of the police station. William removed a knife from his boot and tested the sharpness against the tip of his finger, flinching when they made contact but drawing no blood.

"No, don't stab them." Elizabeth said as she grabbed his wrist and attempted to take the knife off him.

"But they're the enemy." he argued as he slowly lowered the knife and placed it back in his boot

"They are just as much a victim as I was. They just don't know it yet." Elizabeth begged "Trust me, give me the knife, we can do this without hurting anyone." He gave her the knife and walked towards the door, placing his hand on it before turning around and facing the rest of the group.

"Does anyone have a PCD?" he asked as he pointed to the machine on the wall that checked for it on your breath. Elizabeth reached into her pocket and removed it, handing it to William who held it to his mouth and drank it, leaning down and breathing into the machine causing the door to open.

"Masks on." Danni said as she flipped the switch and turned the speaker on letting the words sound before entering the building, the guard ran through them and out of the door looking for the person that opened the door.

Cup of Sleep

"We should kill him." William whispered in Elizabeth's ear.

"He has no idea we are here so what we should do is walk past him and find wherever they keep the communication devices." Danni walked around to the back of his desk and removed from one of the draws a set of keys, placing them in her pocket and joining the rest of the group.

"Follow me." Ramsha said as they carried on ahead, walking into a room connected by an open hallway to the entrance, a block of cells all with open doors, walls cracked and benches damp and mould covered.

"Where are the communication devices?" Elizabeth asked, looking into the cells and attempting to close one of the cell doors only to find it jammed.

"In the basement where they keep the weapons and tea." They passed through to the next room, the staff room, as small as a cupboard containing only two doors and a PCD refiller. They kept walking until in the next room they saw the stairs, descending into the darkened room of the basement, pressing her hand against the wall and feeling her way along it, Elizabeth found the switch and pressed it, the light turning on with a subtle click. They found the wall lined with weapons and communication devices, small boxes of tea of all brands covering the tables and some of the chairs.

153Andrew James King

"Take one." Danni said as William reached up and slid one out of its case, opening the back and checking the battery holder.

"Nothing" he said, taking off his mask and removing the batteries from the speaker, sliding them into the device.

"William and I will distract them," Danni explained. "You and Ramsha need to make your way to the cinnamon factory, it should give you the clearest signal, send the rescue message." The device was given to Ramsha and Danni removed her mask, taking the batteries out and giving them to Elizabeth along with the key to the base. "Get the sleep pod." She requested "get it to my old house and take it to the factory, it is of utmost importance Matulog gets the pod, it's the only way they can recreate it, we can save everyone." She placed the key in Elizabeth's hand and gripped her fingers so tight it felt as though the serrated edge of the key had made her fingers bleed "Promise me you wont get caught, you are the world's last hope." Elizabeth just replied with a silent nod, a reluctant smile spreading across her face and the two parted, William and Danni left first, their masks off running through the station, they heard the yelling of guards and the sound of bullets colliding with metal and wood.

Cup of Sleep

"Should we wait?" Ramsha asked as they took their masks off, breathing deeply and leaning against the wall, Elizabeth doing the same, her forehead dripping with sweat.

"Give it a few seconds." Elizabeth answered, "Just so we can catch our breath." so they waited, Elizabeth and Ramsha sat on the seats they had cleared of tea and spoke.

"Why do you trust us?" Ramsha asked

"What do you mean?" Elizabeth replied

"From what I heard Danni knocked you out, forced you out of the life you knew into this, sitting in the basement of a police station talking to a person you were raised to view as an abomination." They explained.

"You are not an abomination." She smiled "you are who you are and, though she was a terrible person in almost all regards, Mrs. Vanderhep told me to respect that in a person." They both smiled at one another as they waited till it felt right to leave. "How old are you?" Elizabeth asked as she stood up and made her way towards the stairs.

"Didn't it say my age in my file?" Ramsha asked

"Yes but you don't look thirty four" she explained "you do know most people are dead by the time they reach thirty five?"

"I know that," they answered, "but how do you?"

155Andrew James King

Cup of Sleep

"I worked for that company for nearly seventeen years and in that time I have never seen a death report for anyone older than thirty five. You are the oldest person I've gotten a report for and you aren't even a proper citizen of the company, you don't really count given that you've spent most of your life with the rebels. Not dependent on coffee." They made their way up the stairs, past the cells and into the front room, the guard having resumed his post with a cup of coffee in hand, his view blocked by the mug as he drank it.

"To Danni's house." Ramsha said as they pushed the door open and were greeted by the air which felt colder on their still sweat drenched forehead.

Chapter Sixteen
Dreams have shown me who I am

Company policy one thousand eight hundred and twelve: Do not ask questions about The Glass Lady.

Somnus followed them as they both stood in front of the sleep pod, its machinery and lights blinking to life as they opened the pod and placed Charlie inside, he seemed to be more talkative approaching Elizabeth as soon as she opened the door and showing her the picture he had drawn, an image of Benny but the usual buck toothed grin replaced by a frown of either sadness or disappointment.

"It looks so…" Elizabeth began

"Terrible," Somnus added

"Great," Elizabeth said, turning to Somnus and looking her in the eyes "the picture looks great." he took the image and folded it up, placing the now smaller page in his pocket and getting into the pod, in which Elizabeth and Ramsha tightened the straps and closed the lid.

"Why did you lie to him?" Somnus asked

"I didn't lie." Elizabeth replied as a whisper

"It was terrible." Somnus countered "the colouring wasn't even in the lines."

Cup of Sleep

"If I like it or not doesn't matter" Elizabeth countered, "what matters is if he likes it and is proud of it. And it seems both are true." The machine was turned on as slowly he began to drift off to sleep, head lowering and his eyes remaining closed but movement could be seen behind his eyelids. "Can they see you?" Elizabeth asked as Somnus walked up to the pod and began touching the screens, dials and buttons on the side.

"No, only you." she said

"Why me?" Elizabeth asked

"Because you believe." Somnus explained "everyone else sees me as a tool, a figure for their propaganda but you, from a young age you knew I was real no matter how much you tried to deny it, you prevented me being forgotten like by brothers and sisters and for that I am forever grateful."

"Let's go." Ramsha said as they lifted the pod up by the back, tilting it so the wheels were on the ground but nothing else. "Could you get the door?" they asked. Elizabeth ran ahead, holding the doors open as the pod was rolled though until it was in the street. "Where does Danni live?" Elizabeth nodded and walked away, in the direction she knew Danni lived and Ramsha followed the people they passed on the street pausing to look at them passed, rubbing their eyes and then walking away glancing back occasionally.

"Aren't you worried they will report us?" Ramsha asked.

"Do you know what they see?" Elizabeth answered

"No," Ramsha replied

"Neither do I." Elizabeth explained "but what I do know is they have probably seen weirder things. The coffee makes you see things. Strange things."

"Like what?" Ramsha asked, each of their words accompanied by a grunt as the pod moved up and down the rises and falls in the pavement.

"I once saw someone running through the street turning invisible,"Elizabeth explained. "One second they were there and the next they were gone, I saw people fly lifted off the ground by a stream of coffee. Things like that, things that look real at the time but when you think about it afterwards you know they can't be real." Elizabeth looked into the air, to the sun which beat down on them, causing yet more sweat to drip down their faces, Ramsha suffering the worst for it under the weight of the pod.

"Want me to take over?" Elizabeth asked as she placed her hand on the part of the handle Ramsha's hand was not covering.

"Yes please," they replied, their breathing deep and laboured as they stepped to the side, Elizabeth catching the pod by the other side of the handle before it could tip too far and start to fall. They walked, stopping only when they saw Danni's house, a guard at the front of the door drinking a cup of coffee

"Who's there?" He asked once he finished, aiming his gun at them and approaching "What's that?" He looked through the glass of the pod, right at Charlie and pointed his gun at him, the barrel resting against the glass.

"This isn't what it looks like." Elizabeth tried to explain. The guard removed a walkie talkie from his pocket, twisted the dial and spoke into it.

"Possible unproductives at the old Davis residence please advise." For a moment after the request there was silence, the sound of static as they waited for a reply and when it came it was a voice that shocked the guard.

"Let them though." the voice said "they're doing important work for me."

"But madam," the voice on the other side of the radio cringed as he spoke, "they have a sleep pod with a child inside."

"Did I stutter!" the voice on the other side of the radio yelled causing the guard to drop it, bits of plastic and metal breaking apart on the floor, the batteries rolling out of the back

"Go on ahead." the guard instructed holding the door open as the pair walked through it.

"What was that?" Elizabeth asked Ramsha

Cup of Sleep

"I don't know," they replied, "but that voice, it sounded familiar." They walked in front of the pod and cribbed the bottom, lifting it up with the help of Elizabeth and carrying it downstairs.

"Danni said you worked for the police, maybe you've met them before or maybe just heard their voice." Elizabeth suggested

"It's not that. I can only think of one idea but it can't be them, they're dead. Have been for weeks." they stepped down the first step, looking over their shoulder as they did before doing the same with the second, third steps and so on till they were on the flat ground they placed the sleep pod down, Ramsha opening the lid while Elizabeth found the bookcase that hid the passage way, pushing it out of the way and directing Ramsha's attention towards it. Charlie climbed out of the pod and sat next to it, stretching his legs as he leaned against the rounded side.

"Did you sleep well?" Elizabeth asked as he stood up, but before he could answer he looked around the room, seeing where he was and looking up at Elizabeth.

"Am I home?" he asked looking around the darkened room, through where the bookshelf used to be and deep into the tunnel.

"Yes," Ramsha confirmed "but we can't stay here for long." They helped him to his feet, his arm over their shoulder as they approached the tunnel but Elizabeth did not follow, she just stood there looking at the chair on which Somnus sat. "What's wrong?"

"Nothing," Elizabeth answered. "Just go on ahead, I'll catch up later, there's something I need to do here." Wordlessly the pair made their way through the tunnel, Elizabeth approaching the chair Somnus sat on and sat on one she moved so they were sitting face to face.

"I know everything about you." Somnus said unprompted "Yet there's one thing that has always confused me about you."

"What's that?" Elizabeth asked

"Given everything that happened to you, why did you support them?" Somus asked "they have done some awful things in the name of profit yet you did everything they said and not out of fear."

"I believed the ends justified the means." Elizabeth answered with a sigh, "That no matter what they did it was okay because they were leading the charge, they were rebuilding the world."

"What changed?" Somnus asked

"I used the sleep pod, when the hallucinations ended, I saw that the world had been rebuilt decades ago, probably before I was even born." With a wave of Somnus' hand the world around them changed, they were no longer in the darkened basement long since abandoned.

zZZ

Eighteen years earlier

They were in a museum, looking through a glass case at an old woman who sat motionless on a chair, *The Glass Lady* written on the tablet in front of the case. Somnus nowhere to be seen.

"That's just a robot you know?" A voice behind her said as it stepped forward to be at her side.

"Shut up Jane." Elizabeth found herself saying without intending to "She's real, The Glass Lady is real." She was ten again, Jane at her side as they walked through the museum of war.

"Why do you think she only talks when you press the button?" Jane asked as she leaned forward and presson the button underneath the table that caused The Glass Lady to talk.

"Good evening young ladies." she said, each word sounding like a labour "Do you have any questions about before the war?" The pair of friends looked at each other.

"How did people get anything done if everyone was an unproductive?" the question seemed to make her wince.

"There were people at the time who lived similar to how we do now, shunning the actions of the unproductive in the name of progress, fuling themselves with nothing but coffee but they did not have the conviction of us now, even they would sleep. But they did work, not because they wanted to but because they knew they must." She slumped over again, having answered the question.

"Told you she's just a robot." Jane said, but Elizabeth saw something else, a thin line of red dripping from the armrest of her left hand, dripping into the bottom of the case and through a drain disappearing off somewhere. Elizabeth pressed her nose against the glass, watching almost hypnotised as the red dropped from the old woman's finger rolling down the arm of the chair and onto the floor.

"What do you think is behind it?" Jane asked

"Why don't you ask?" Elizabeth replied

"No," Jane answered, "you ask." Their class had long since abandoned them and they heard the calls of Mrs. Vanderhep who wandered from exhibit to exhibit jumping as some of the animatronics came to life.

"Fine." Elizabeth said as she walked away and approached the door, being stopped by one of the guards.

"Can we help you?" He asked.

"What's in there?" Elizabeth asked, pointing to the door and attempting to reach for the handle.

Cup of Sleep

"Some very important machinery." the guard said as he gently grabbed her wrist and lowered it.

"Can I see it?" Elizabeth asked

"I'm sorry little girl but you can't" the guard explained before resuming his post and ignoring all further questions. Elizabeth made her way back to a disappointed looking Jane.

"Better luck next time." Elizabeth said as she walked away, stopping when she heard loud footsteps from behind, Jane had ran towards the guard, kicking him in the shin and forced the door open, Elizabeth following behind walking and stepping over the guard who lay on the floor hand on knee, Jane had opened the door and was nearly blinded by the light within the otherwise dark room; an audio recorder next to a microphone though they could not hear what the recorder was saying they knew it was playing something. Elizabeth approached and with a single click turned the audio recording off, the world around her changed, holes in the walls fading and being filled in, the surrounding rubble no longer there, getting smaller and smaller with each blink.

"What's going on?" Elizabeth asked as she was around her, the building repairing itself, then ran from the room, seeing all the museum guests reaching for random spots on the ground and trying to stick their hands through the wall where there once was a hole. The guard stood up, running into the room and pressing the button, the world around them sliding back into place like paint not yet dried on a wall. The pair ran, finding Mrs. Vanderhep by the exit holding the door open with her foot.

"Where have you two been?" she asked as the rest of the students filed out "I have been worried about you."

"I'm sorry Vanderhep." the pair said at once

"We were talking to The Glass Lady." Jane explained as they got onto the bus and went home.

zZZ

"Your dreams have shown me who you are." Somnus declared "Or at least who you were." She stood up and made her way to the tunnel. " Curious woman, and in a world like this that makes you a danger to yourself."

Chapter Seventeen
Coffee Liqueur

Company policy six hundred and eight: In times of celebration when a break from work is allowed the only alcohol that may be consumed is coffee liqueurs.

The first thing Elizabeth heard when she entered the factory was the music, the noise blaring through the thick walls as Ramsha continued to set up the sleep pod, tapping one of the many screens. "What was that about?" they asked as they walked away from the pod and sat down.

"I can see her." Elizabeth explained also taking a seat.

"See who?" Ramsha asked

"Somnus," Elizabeth explained "ever since I was a child I've seen her, always in the background but then When I used the sleep pod, she started talking to me." She stood up again and approached the stairs, lifting her ear up and finding the source of the music to be nearby, the sounds of music, cheering and the smashing of bottles thrown against a hollow metal surface echoing down into the otherwise silent room.

"What does she say?" Ramsha asked.

Cup of Sleep

"I don't know, it's different each time. Before she was asking why I continued to support Benny, she showed me something I had forgotten, I was friends with the person who got Sarah killed." She grabbed the communication device and made her way up the stairs, her hands running along the rusted railing and up passing doors and windows as she heard no music through them until she found one door that had no window, just a solid slab of metal with a door handle. She pushed it open and was immediately overwhelmed by the smell of coffee, overwhelmed because there was something else to it, something she didn't recognise until a cup of the stuff was shoved into her hand by a passing worker. Still in uniform but lacking the vacant expression of the last time she was in the factory she took a sip. It tasted mostly of coffee, a taste that now made her wince with disgust, but that didn't happen this time. It felt cold as she drank it with a subtle sweetness to it that she could not place yet she took one more step into the room, the music sounding like it was coming from all sides of the room, dead bodied shoved into the corner, her face plus the face of Danni, William and Ramsha on a large screen hanging over the room on the far wall, yet as she went further into the room no one seemed to recognise her, each of their steps made with great effort as to not trip over their one feet.

Cup of Sleep

"Welcome to the party pal," one of the men said as they approached her and held his drink up to her they toasted, the man cheering upon collision yelling "to their failure." he laughed as he downed his drink in two gulps.

"I'm sorry," Elizabeth asked, "Who's failing?" She took a sip of her drink and despite her new found disliking of coffee actually enjoyed the taste.

"The terrorists of course." he laughed "there was a whole plot to get a bunch of them away from us but we stopped them. Bang!" The last part a yell loud enough to be heard over the music and draw the attention of people surrounding them "I hear one of them was even shot in the face." A low chuckle could be heard under the music.

"Leave her alone," a man in a mask said as he approached, taking her hand and kissing it "Can't you see the lady is startled by your…" he paused "unique personality."

"It's not my fault she's not as merry as I." he said as he walked away to a small group of workers who were drinking and taking bets.

"Thank you for the rescue," she said to the stranger who's masked face showed only a grin on his exposed mouth,

"Twice you've been here and twice I've needed to save you," he said as he removed the mask and revealed the face of William, taking his cup and having a drink. "I'm starting to think you shouldn't be here."

"Where's Danni?" Elizabeth asked as William led her to the centre of the room and they started dancing, Elizabeth resting her head against William's shoulder.

"She needed some time with her family," he explained "said she would be done in about five minutes, told me to find you and make sure you don't do anything stupid."

"Did she really say that?" Elizabeth laughed as they went into a spin, the dance continuing despite the change of song.

"Most of it," he answered, "I added the last bit." for a second they parted, both Elizabeth and William stopping the dance to have a bit of their drink. "What is this stuff?" he asked as he took another sip and the pair began dancing again, this time with no music, stopping when someone got on stage and static bleared from the microphone

"I'm sorry to say the DJ has died." Four people in gas masks walked up to the body and picked it up, one limb per person and walked into the corner throwing it down and resuming the party as another person wearing similar clothes took the DJ's place.

Cup of Sleep

"Do you have the communication device?" William asked, watching as she reached into her pocket and removed it, placing it in his hands.

"Wanna go now?" She asked as she continued to have her drink with everyone else.

"Not yet." he explained "we should probably wait for the party to be over, it's best to send the message when it's as quiet as possible." They continued dancing, throughout the night, occasionally swapping partners but doing their best to stay together.

"I think you left something here Mrs. Black." one of her partners said as they danced to a song slow dancing was not appropriate for

"What do you mean?" she asked

"Your uniform, you put it in your locker then you left." he explained as they swapped partners, back with William.

"Glad to have you back." he said "I was worried he recognised you." his head gestured to the giant screen going further and further back as they turned to the point he had to swap which side he was looking at it from the other side.

"I don't think they are at the top of their senses." she said as she accidentally stepped on the foot of someone passing by, for a moment he said nothing just drinking and going back to his partner until all at once he yelled out in pain, not an intense pain but loud enough for Elizabeth to hear.

"I think this drink is alcoholic." she said as she pushed her drink further away until someone hit the table, causing it to spill on the floor.

"You know what?" William began "I think you're right." He did the same as they backed away from them and walked to the other side of the room towards the door.

"We should probably head to the roof." Elizabeth suggested and William agreed pushing the door open and continuing through the building up a set of stains until they she went to open one more she felt the coolness of the night air through the gap as with one push she saw the moon hanging full in the air, heard footsteps behind them that doubled as they sped up, Danni and Ramsha appeared, drinks in hand.

"Are you ready to send the message?" Ramsha asked as they placed their cup on the ground by their feet.

"Almost," William answered "first we need to wait for the music to stop, get a clear signal so we know they will receive it."

"And spell the name correctly this time," Elizabeth laughed as she handed Danni the communication device, William laughed as well

"Oh yeah, how did you spell it last time?" he asked knowing the answer already "m u t o o l o o g" Danni answered looking over to Ramsha who was laughing quietly to themselves "Ramsha doesn't know what happened." Elizabeth realised

"Alex certainly found it funny." William explained

"How about Ramsha and I will go back and find some way to sabotage the speakers," Elizabeth suggested "I'll tell them what happened."

$$zZ$$

Elizabeth was standing on Ramsha's cupped hands, her hands on their shoulders using them as a step ladder to reach up to one of the wires and, reaching into her boot to remove William's knife, cut the wire in half, doing her best to avoid the exposed wiring.

"What happened with the first message?" Ramsha asked as they lowered Elizabeth to the ground and they made their way to the other side of the room, repeating the process

"When Danni sent the first message she misspelled the name of the resistance movement, I had a good laugh about it and it seems William did as well, that message is the reason he's here." with the second wire cut they could hear the music get quieter and moved on to the next wire.

"And probably Alex as well," Ramsha confirmed "they see all messages from the outside to make sure they aren't traps."

"Who is Alex?" Elizabeth asked as she used the metal beams keeping the speaker attached to the wall to keep her balance.

"What do you mean?" Ramsha asked.

"People have mentioned their name many times before but haven't asked who they are." Elizabeth cut the fourth wire, the music coming solely from one speaker on the other side of the room yet people danced like before. Elizabeth looked over the crowd and saw that it had nearly halved since she had last been in the room, the amount of bodies stacked in the corner having increased drastically as to nearly outnumber the people who were still alive. With one final climb, one final slice of the knife there was silence, the speakers dead on the walls as Elizabeth and Ramsha looked around and saw people still dancing, their moves clumsy and out of sync with their partners but they were trying to keep up with each other.

"They can still hear the music." Ramsha said, the pair wandered through the crowd seeming invisible to the eyes around them, they just danced.

Cup of Sleep

"Hello?" Elizabeth called out standing in front of the man who had welcomed her to the party.

"I'm sorry!" The man yelled "this music is too loud I can hardly hear you!" he danced away, joining back up with the men drinking and betting, louder this time for the music seemed to them almost deafening. The pair looked at each other.

"Back to the room?" Ramsha asked as they began to walk to the stair that led that way.

"Agreed." Elizabeth said as she followed, breathing in deeply as the cool air of the night brushed against her face, until that moment she had not realised how much she was sweating.

"Have you sent the message?" Ramsha asked as they reached into their pocket and took out a tissue, passing it to Elizabeth for her to wipe her brow.

"Not yet," Danni answered, "we just need to find the right receiver." There was a moment of near silence, the only sound being the ticking and beeping of the machine as the direction it faced was adjusted. "Got it!" she exclaimed as the screen went from an almost completely faded grey to a bright green, the words signal received flashing on and off.

"May I?" William asked, reaching his hand out, awaiting the communication device.

"You may," Danni said, passing it to him, "but make sure you spell it properly." he took the device and pressed a button on the side causing a small keyboard to pop out of the bottom and began typing, saying it out loud.

"Mayday," he began "Mayday, we have been exposed. Requesting immediate evacuation from the cinnamon factory, searching for Somnus." once the message was sent the device began to spark, the sindies heating up to the point where a faint glow could be seen between the seams which held the casing together causing William to drop it.

"What now?" Elizabeth asked

"Now, we wait." Danni answered.

Chapter Eighteen
Order Up

Company policy four hundred twenty nine: attendance at the opening of a new exhibit in the museum of coffee is mandatory as part of a strict loyalty exercise.

They marked the passage of time with the beeping of coffee reminders, taking breaks every half an hour, two beeps, and sending someone into the factory to steal food from the fridge in the staff room.

"What sort of person puts coffee beans on a ham sandwich?" Ramsha asked as he removed the top layer of bread and scraped the now powder-like beans off the dry meat.

"Someone who needs coffee to survive," Elizabeth reminded them "I used to season my eggs with coffee grinds and have one with the sandwich, call it brown eggs and ham."

"Says it belongs to a Claire Black," Danni confirmed as she picked up the box and read the name on top "that's a name I never thought I'd hear again."

"Do you know her?" Ramsha asked

"Not directly," Danni confirmed, raising her hand to point at Elizabeth who was eating a cheese sandwich "but this one pretended to be her when she was first here, stole the uniform right out of her locker."

"No," Elizabeth contested "you stole the uniform and gave it to me, my hands are clean. Except for this sandwich, far too much butter." after finishing their food, placing the wrappers in a bag and hiding it in the corner Danni went off to check the pod, Ramsha stood guard at the door and William started making everyone a cup of tea with the bag he gathered from the police station

"Do you wanna talk about what happened at the dance?" he asked as he poured the boiled water over the bags.

"What do you mean?" Elizabeth asked as she took the milk out of the fridge and started adding it to the cups.

"The dance," William answered, "you resting your head against my neck and smiling like that, I know you felt something." he started adding sugar to the drinks.

"I'd be lying if I said I didn't," she answered with a faint smile on her face, taking her drink in hand and having a sip. "But I think Danni likes you and I don't want to do anything to hurt her, I think I've done enough of that already."

"Is this about Sarah?" William asked as he took a sip of his drink, putting the rest on a tray placing a bit of card with the names of the remaining members on "you do know she doesn't blame you, she blames Jane and the police officer that shot her. Plus I don't think Charlie could blame you, not a hateful bone in his body." the pair laughed, "Says he sees Somnus following you which in our line of work is the highest compliment you could give someone." Tray in hand he waked towards Ramsha, leaving Elizabeth alone to approach Charlie, sitting at his side and messing with his hair.

"Hey dude," she said, placing her cup on the table "how are you doing?"

"I'm good," he answered "Look what I drew?" he said shifting a piece of paper in front of them, it was a drawing of a factory, the smoke coming out of the chimney a brownish colour, five people standing in front of it, four holding hands with one off to the side.

"This looks great," the people were all stick figures wearing only one item to tell them apart. "Can I ask you a question?" Elizabeth asked to which Charlie replied with a nod "How many people do you see in this room?" she asked.

"six" Charlie answered, "me, you, mom, William, Ramsha and Somnus, the woman that follows you everywhere." without moving Elizabeth felt breathing on her neck, heard it as well deep and spaced out. She turned showly and saw, now on the other side of the room.

"You can see her?" Elizabeth asked, gesturing towards her with her head.

Cup of Sleep

"Yes," he answered "I thought I was the only one, I saw her first when you came to talk about dad, on the other side of the street. I think she's following you."

"Smart kid." Somnus said, suddenly sitting in the chair next to Elizabeth, sipping her tea though its continents never went down.

"How can you see her?" Elizabeth asked, not turning her head to look at Somnus yet it was she who answered.

"Because he believes, all the children of Matulog believe. To the adults I am a propaganda tool, to them I am the guardian that protects them as they sleep. Parents tell them stories of me as they sleep." she leaned in closer and whispered "most of them are untrue."

"So I am the only adult that can see you?" Elizabeth asked.

"Pretty much." Somnus answered, "Yet you don't really see me, you see the me you believe in. You see the me on the posters and described in the horror stories played on the radio as you worked your daily grind, I used to be a man before the propaganda started depicting me in this body." before she could continue Danni approached, sitting in the same seat Somnus was sitting in causing her to fade away like a puff of smoke leaving only Danni in her place.

"I had an idea." she began.

Cup of Sleep

"What sort of idea?" Elizabeth asked

"The resistance will be here in two days, give or take depending on weather," Danni explained "So I'm thinking we may not be able to fake their deaths but we can still save someone."

"That's great!" Elizabeth exclaimed as she got out of her seat. "Who?" Danni took from her pocket the list of names and placed it on the table.

"Name Esther Weston, pronouns she/they, lives about ten minutes away from here and is unfortunately under investigation. We need to help them."

"Ok," Elizabeth responded, "What do you need me to do?"

"Do you remember how you announced your return the first time during the celebration of seventeen seventy three?" she asked as she reached into her pocket and pulled out a map.

"Yeah," Elizabeth answered "I got on stage and told everyone but you may be forgetting I was captured pretty much immediately."

"William will be there to make sure that doesn't happen," Danni assured "but what we need you to do is draw their attention. She is the doctor that keeps The Glass Lady alive, but the main base is running out of doctors, we need them back not only to be a doctor but to be a teacher." The map she laid on the table was one of the museum, one large room, the many cases marked with what's in them, surrounded by several smaller rooms unlabeled but with a number ranging from one to five.

"A new exhibit is opening up about the signing of the bill that made sleep illegal. I think that is the best time to strike, when everyone attending will be in the same room. According to the museum's website The Glass Lady will be out of service for a medical check up, if we get her there we can slip them out the back."

"Is there anything I should be aware of before I go?" Elizabeth asked.

"Just that we will probably run into Jane and Harold, just keep your head down and cover as much of your body as you can." Elizabeth nodded and took a deep breath, "Are you ready?" Danni asked.

"Yes." Elizabeth replied.

$$zZZ$$

She wore a gas mask, a pair of workers overalls and rubber gloves as she entered the museum, they patted her down, checking each of her pockets as she passed through the metal detector and came out the otherside into the largest room of the museum the stage set up in the middle, the only thing delaying the speech being a group of sound engineers, people had already started dying, dragged out of the room and piled up in one of the rooms she remembered being labelled one.

"Is there anything I can help you with?" one of the museum staff asked as she presented Elizabeth with a pamphlet, a smile that did not reach her eye marking her face.

"Do you know how long till the speech begins?" she asked as she unfolded it, using it to cover her face as she saw more people enter the museum.

"Shouldn't take too long, maybe five minutes." The guide walked away to a couple that had called her name. Elizabeth looked around and saw the case The Glass Lady was supposed to be kept in was empty. For the first time she saw the arm rest, saw a hole in the end of it, she pressed the button and saw a small, blood-coated spike strike out of it before quickly sinking back down. Her thought process was interrupted by the sound of microphone static as an ageing man approached the microphone and said five words

"Testing testing, one, two, three," and a silence washed over the room. She turned and saw William, Danni and Ramsha sneak into one of the back rooms.

"Ladies, gentlemen and other," the whole room bursted out in laughter before he could continue, "In all seriousness, ladies and gentlemen I welcome you to the

183Andrew James King

opening of this, an exhibit about the transition times." They began passing drinks and mini bites to eat around to everyone in the room. "We have been asked many times why we didn't make one for this before, why has it taken so long and now I will tell you," he looked down, a single forced tear rolling from his eye "unfortunately the memory of that day is still too fresh in my mind, but no more I decided, I decided to give this gift unto you. My people. The gift of the truth." Before the curtain could be opened, the exhibit shown to everyone, Elizabeth took the bread roll she had been handed and threw it at the stage, striking the old man in the back of the head, drawing everyone's attention as she approached, removing her mask and ascending the steps. "Who are you?" the old man asked, "I demand to know!" with a mocking bow Elizabeth introduced herself "My name is Elizabeth Clair, perhaps you've heard of me." Then he smiled, a small knowing smile, one filled not with arrogance or greed but memory, nostalgia.

"I guess your mother was right," he said so low that only she could hear "you can't keep a claire down for long." Elizabeth reached blinded to the side, feeling around for the stand that held the microphone picked up and swung, stopping an inch away from his face as one of his guards grabbed it and pulled taking her throat in one hand and squeezing, but not for long as a sandbag fell from the rafters, landing on his head and causing him to fall to the floor.

"We've got them!" Willam yelled from above "Run!" Elizabeth swung her fist, connecting with the old man's face and dropping down from the stage running for the door but stopping as a hand latched onto her wrist, throwing her against the wall and picking her up, dragging her by her neck into one of the side rooms, locking it behind her. A small room appeared to be under construction as one of the walls was just a thin sheet of wood.

"Bet you didn't expect to see me." Jane said as she kicked Elizabeth in the ribs winding her.

"Actually I was surprised I hadn't seen you sooner." she struggled to say.

"This is no time for jokes!" Jane yelled

"Do you remember when we were here?" Elizabeth asked as she struggled to her feet, watching as Jane paused mid swing.

"What do you mean?" Jane asked

"We were here when we were younger," Elizabeth answered, "with Mrs. Vanderhep." Elizabeth could see her struggling to remember something. "We were standing by The Glass Lady and you were telling me you thought she was a robot." Jane paused for a moment looking into Elizabeth's eyes.

Cup of Sleep

"You betrayed us." Jane yelled running at her, wrapping her arms around Elizabeth's waist and slamming her through the wood, they fell together, past piping and wiring, blinded by the sawdust as they landed on the stony ground three floors beneath where they once stood. Elizabeth landed on top of Jane, the only sign of life being the slow rising and falling of her chest. Elizabeth searched the body and found her PCD, filling one of the nearby buckets with it and leaving it by her head, walking away hoping she would survive.

186Andrew James King

Chapter Nineteen
Steam

Company policy one hundred and thirty: the source of Byritherol must not be discovered.

The pipes around Elizabeth seemed alive, breathing out the steam which caused sweat to drip off her forehead and hands which she attempted to dry on the side of her clothes in vain. She ran down the hallway as fast as she could despite the pain in her side, the sound of her own heart beating in her head because despite knowing it was just her own footsteps echoing through the maze-like corridors, she felt as though someone was following her. "Hello!" she yelled, listening as the sound reflected back before disappearing, leaving only the sound of the water as it dripped from the ceiling and joined with the puddles then built up along the floor. Eventually the pain became too much for her, the pain in her chest like someone had grabbed her heart and squeezed.

"You lost?" a voice echoed from every side "Stay right where you are, I'll find you." she found part of the wall that wasn't covered in pipes and leaned against it, sliding down the wall and sitting in a puddle, she soon found herself sobbing

187Andrew James King

Cup of Sleep

"It's okay." the voice said "I'll find you and lead you to the workstation and then everything will be okay." A moment of silence passed, the only sound being the pounding of heavy work boots against stone.

"What's your name?" Elizabeth called out before she could stop herself, she slammed her hand against her mouth

"Edith." the woman called out "What's yours?" for a brief moment Elizabeth went quiet before calling out "Claire. My name is Claire Black."

"Listen, we saw the fall, I need you to try and stay awake so I'm gonna ask you some questions and I want you to do your best to answer them." with the adrenalin fading Elizabeth could feel her grip on reality slipping.

"Yeah, I understand." she replied

"Ok, Claire, how old are you?" she asked

"Im…I'm twenty eight."

"A youngin I see," she joked

"No, I'm pra…practically on death's door." keeping her eyelids open became a chore.

"Next question, how do you like your coffee?" she asked, her breathing becoming more laboured.

"I normally had it with three coffee spoons of sugar," Elizabeth explained "but there was an incident at work, I got one of my co-workers orders, he had his with caramel."

Cup of Sleep

"No more questions, I've found you." The last thing Elizabeth saw before the darkness was a woman in a workers uniform running towards her, eyes not marked by the dark rings of tiredness, hands perfectly still, her teeth unstained then she was overwhelmed by the darkness and the feeling of nothingness.

zZZ

Elizabeth awoke for a moment and saw she was being carried, cradled, in the arms of a stranger running through the darkness unaware that the person she was carrying was awake yet still she spoke "It's gonna be okay," she whispered "were gonna get you to the doctor, she'll get a good look at you." They came to a halt in front of a heavy looking vault door as she was placed on the ground, a keycard removed from her pocket and swiped it along a machine beside the typing in a code Elizabeth could not see. Then the darkness claimed her again. The only thing she could hear was the intense beeping of the alarms as the door slid open and the smell in the air changed from stagnant water to a mix of petrel and oil.

zZZ

189189Andrew James King

Cup of Sleep

It took a moment for her eyes to adjust, the harsh light of the hospital room greeting her as she regained consciousness and began sitting up overwhelmed by a headache, the world spinning around her. A hand rested against her shoulder and moved one of her pillows so she could sit up in bed "she's awake," the person yelled, looking at the door until it opened and Edith walked in.

"Is she okay?" Edith asked.

"She's only just woken up so I don't know for sure." the doctor answered, "I'm calling you in to fill in some of the gaps the patient may have."

"Clair." Elizabeth croaked "My name is Claire Black."

"Ah, yes," the doctor remarked as she picked up the clipboard from the end of the bed and unfolded it "So, Claire, how did you end up in our neck of the woods?" she asked.

"Would you believe me if I told you I fell?" Elizabeth laughed "Right from the museum to here, Quite the drop would not recommend." The doctor took a few steps back and turned to face the medicine cabinet.

"There's a museum?" she asked as she removed a box of painkillers "This should help with the headache." She gave Elizabeth two of them plus a cup of water but she took both without drinking it, choking but eventually getting them down. "The water does help you swallow them." the doctor said.

"I'd rather not." Elizabeth said. Feeling the world around her stop spinning, her headache subsiding, Elizabeth stood up balancing on her bed and reaching for the door.

"I wouldn't do that if I were you." Edith said, grabbing her by the shoulder and leading her to a chair. "You're in the hospital wing now but you are not authorised to see what's on the other side of that door, the guards won't allow it." She attempted to pull the curtains over the window but found them stuck.

"What do you do here?" she asked

"We make Byritherol," she answered "we don't know what it does but they put our grandparents in here and told them they couldn't leave but new people will be sent down."

"So you've never been outside?" Elizabeth asked

"Not a single one of us has seen what I believe you call the sun," Edith answered.

"How will I get out?" None of them replied but their silence spoke volumes. "I won't." Elizabeth answered defeated.

"I'm sorry." The doctor said in a similar defeated tone. "You're one of us now." Standing up, her balance now fully restored, Elizabeth ran for the door and pushed, running through it and into the larger part of the factory without difficulty stopping when she looked out into the open space and saw the machines. Giant metal chairs lined the edge of the walls and in neat rows running from one end of the room to the other, plastic tubes flowing with blood sticking out of every limb. The heart rate monitors at their sides almost flatlined except the occasional spike which appeared for a brief moment and then disappeared again. Elizabeth just stood there watching, hands rested on the yellow railing, the only thing that stopped her falling.

"I can't stay here." she said as Edith approached from behind

"But you have to," she replied "if you leave they will kill you."

"I have to try," Elizabeth continued, "there are people waiting for me." She looked around, seeing the factory poorly maintained, the guards patrolling the walkways which hung above the factory.

"If you run they will kill you." Edith pleaded as Elizabeth looked around the room again and saw a door, old and untouched .

"They will most certainly try." she smiled running past as quick as she could reaching out for the handle and finding herself back into the darkness, shouts echoing behind her.

"She's escaping," the first one cried.

Cup of Sleep

"She knows the secret," went the second one

"She cannot get out alive." the final one yelled as she ran down the stony hall, ducking and weaving as the pipes spat out steam, holes punctured in the metal by the bullets which flew past her head as she ran only stopping when she found a dead end attempting to turn around but falling to the ground as bullets flew past again, missing by mere inches.

"We have you surrounded!" one of them yelled "come out with your hands up or your death will be painful." Elizabeth closed her eyes and did not give them the satisfaction of a response.

"What mess have you gotten yourself in." Somnus smiled as she sat down behind the ruble.

"The three little pigs here," Elizabeth mocked, "want to shoot me." She reached to her side and picked up a rocking, throwing it over her head, over the rubble and heard as the gun shots fired and the rock hit the floor.

"I suppose now is as good a time as any to finish the story." as with a wave of her hand the world around her began to melt

"What story?" she asked as the dark damp tunnels around her became an open field.

"The story of the man you punched." she joked as the man appeared and with him the statue, that eldritch abomination that saw everything, even her dreams.

Cup of Sleep

"The man you punched was Richard Michelson. Great grandson of the founder of the Benny Beans coffee company." they were now in the middle of the city, one not marked or ruined by the violence of war.

"Why did he do it?" Elizabeth asked as she approached who did not move.

"I believe his intentions were good," she answered "to begin with anyway." he began to move but showed no sign he knew they were there.

"How is rebuilding going?" he asked his secretary

"Sir," he seemed almost hesitant to answer but eventualy he fought against his restraint and answered "it's finished."

"What do you mean?" Richard asked

"A great burden has been lifted," his secretary answered "and now the Benny Beans coffee company can go back to what it was before."

"Do you know what we were before this?"

"No," was the answer "I joined during this mess."

"We were nothing," Richard answered the unasked question "Just one of several in a market so over-saturated there's one on every street."

"But we have served our purpose," his secretary pleaded, "please sir, people are dying. They need sleep." Without replying Richard walked away, stepping into one of the boots of the statue and taking his phone out and

194Andrew James King

dialling a number, Elizabeth found herself in the lift with him.

"Come on," he begged, looking at his phone and waiting for the person to pick up.

"Michel." he said as soon as they did, putting it on speaker and turning the volume up as loud as possible

"Yes sir," Michel responded. "How may I help you?" with newfound authority he spoke

"We need speakers," Richard ordered "and we need them now."

"How many?" Michel asked

"As many as possible," Richard told him "we need them scattered as far and wide as we can and we need as many people as possible to hear them." The elevator stopped at his office at the very tip of the statue, the world around them melting leaving behind only the darkened hallway Elizabeth had nearly forgotten about. Her slow fade into reality quickened by the sound of gunshots causing her to scream, but she did not see them hit the wall anywhere near her, the sparks as they grazed the walls or the pipes that hissed with steam she heard the screams of others, and then as quick as they had started they ended. Sher found herself back in the tunnels.

"You can come out now." one of the survivors called out to her.

Cup of Sleep

"Who are you?" Elizabeth asked, turning her head and seeing a group of four people in dark uniforms, holding guns with flashlights on the ends.

"I'm dropping my gun." one of them called out followed by a loud thud and a splash "we mean you no harm, I am approaching slowly." One of the people in dark uniforms approached and sat on the floor in front of her, removing their mask and showing their face. It was beautiful; their green eyes staring into Elizabeth's as she prepared to introduce herself, her skin almost as dark as the uniform she wore contrasting the brightness of her blond hair, they smiled showing a row of crooked teeth and said in an unplaceable accent.

"My name is Alex Shoulder, I've been told a lot about you. It's a pleasure to meet you."

Epilogue
A New Day

Despite everything around her, the bed specifically made for her, the locks on the doors and the general knowledge that it was safe to sleep, Elizabeth lay awake at what she believed to be two in the morning staring at the ceiling of the room that felt both too small and too big. The room was sparsely decorated, just a bed with plain white sheets, a desk scattered with paper, pens and rulers and a plastic chair softened by the spare pillow she had been given. As she attempted to get back to sleep she heard a knock at the door, a face she had never seen before looking through the glass, its pale eyes scanning the room. "Open." Elizabeth said as she adjusted her pillow so she could sit up, a soft buzz followed by the sound of the door opening and closing.

"Can't sleep?" she asked as they took a seat on the end of the bed, watching as Elizabeth shook her head.

"Neither can I." the figure laughed, "It's these beds." she said, pushing their hand into the mattress and letting it sink up to her wrist.

"Yeah," Elizabeth agreed. "It's too soft, worried if I stay in it too long it's gonna swallow me whole." They both laughed awkwardly.

197Andrew James King

Cup of Sleep

"Wanna go for a walk?" Esther asked as she got up and approached the door "You have a busy day tomorrow so I'd recommend some sort of sleep remedy. How about a nice glass of warm milk?" Elizabeth tossed her blanket to the side, shivering at the sudden cold and hung her feet off the side of her bed.

"Could you please pass my slippers?" She asked Esther who did, reaching into the wardrobe and removing a pair of fluffy grey slippers, sliding them under Elizabeth's feet. "What is happening tomorrow?" Elizabeth asked as she put the slippers on and stood up, stretching her arms and legs to clear the stiffness of unuse.

"Follow me," Esther said as they left the room, waiting by the side of the door and waiting for Elizabeth to follow her.

"You're lucky," they told Elizabeth.

"How so?" Elizabeth asked.

"You have the blessing and assurances of me, Danni, William and Ramsha." she explained "Anyone would kill for one of them to help but you got all four. Which means you don't need to be tested, you just need to be debriefed. Tomorrow you will be asked a few questions about what happened, your answers will be written down and then you will have free reign of the base when they finish but for now you must have someone walk with you." They reached into the fridge and removed a carton of milk, taking two mugs from a nearby cupboard and filling both half way and throwing it into the microwave. "I'd like to thank you." Esther said, the hum of the microwave sounding in the background.

"What for'?" Elizabeth asked.

"Danni told me everything." she answered "everything you risked in the museum, the fall and how they found you fearing for your life seconds away from being shot. You did that for all of us." when the microwave was finished, the mugs retrieved the pair raising them, placing the heated ceramic against their lips and drank, Elizabeth could already feel sleep wash over her again

"Thank you for this." Elizabeth said once she finished her cup.

"Alex seems to trust you." Esther said, "before they even saw you or spoke to the others, your name seemed familiar to them, Do you know why?"

"No," Elizabeth answered, "the first time I saw their name was on a death notification, it was the one I signed before all this started, I thought they were dead."

"If you thought that," Esther began, "then it means everyone else does, they think we are leaderless." a contemplative look covered their face. "I have a feeling there will be great change in the future, change you have brought about."

Cup of Sleep

"What sort of change?" Elizabeth asked

"I suggest you get back to bed." Esther said, a gentle smile spreading across their face as silently Elizabeth agreed following as she was lead back to her room, door opening the door with a buzz and she was once again alone, the only other living thing being the feeling of Somnus as she lay down, covering her herself with the blanket and let her eyes close. She did not dream that night, but her sleep was not full of turmoil. She merely closed her eyes and waited for what faced her on this, a new day. For the first time in her life she had found true Somnus, the nothing between night and day that healed all wounds, ready again for battle.

200Andrew James King

Bonus

Features

201Andrew James King

A Treaty of Humans and Elves sample
Welcome to Anderfel

Evergreen 1:1: In the beginning, there was Ptfrt and vjspd and a bloody battle which filled the endless nothing with such brilliant light.

The snow around Issac's head turned a deep shade of crimson red as the blood poured from the open wound on his face, but he felt no pain, only numbness as the creature on his back pushed his face further and further into the snow, its tongue digging deeper and deeper into the top of his spine. Suddenly he was in a bar, the sun reflecting through the closed window into his eyes blinding him but he did not need to see to know where he was or who he was with. "Alex?" Issac asked, reaching his hand to the middle of the table.

"Yes my love," His boyfriend replied as their hands met in the middle, Isaac was shocked by how warm Alex's hand felt, "Why are you so cold?" Alex asked as he began to rub Issac's hands. Ignoring his question, Issac looked around and saw the rustic wooden chairs, deers heads hanging from the wall and the bar staff whose expressions ranged from anger to apathy and he immediately knew where they were.

202202Andrew James King

Cup of Sleep

"We've been here before," Issac said, their hands parting as drinks and food were placed in front of him, yet he couldn't smell any of it. As he took his first bite he found himself in the snow again, his face so covered in blood and the water which used to be frozen around him that he could only see out of one eye. "Help!" he screamed, not knowing when, or if he would be rescued.

"How long have we been together?" Alex asked as he found himself back in the bar.

"Seven years," Issac answered as he stabbed his fork into his stew, feeling as if the heads on the wall were watching him.

"Exactly, and after all this time I feel like I'm ready," Issac saw a hand move through the pocket of his jeans and remove something, but before he could see what the snow and the coldness reclaimed his face, a pair of boots standing just a few metres away, joined by several more each with bows drawn.

"Will you marry me?" Alex asked as he got down on one knee and presented the unopened box.

"Yes!" Issac exclaimed as he wrapped his arms out his now fiance's neck and tackled him to the ground with a hug, kissing all over his face before focusing on the lips.

"You haven't even opened the box." he laughed as he fumbled to his side reaching for the thing he had dropped, handing it back to Issac.

"There is not a gem or jewel I would like to look at now more than the ones in your eyes." Issac flirted as he took the box back and opened it, not seeing the ring he remembered, the one whose shadow he could feel on his finger. The deer heads on the wall turned to face him, a green liquid pouring from their eyes as they screamed. He saw an arrowhead, the one he now saw impaling the snow-covered ground in front of him killing the monster.

Interview Questions

1.What inspired you to start writing?

The biggest factor that made me want to start writing was honestly boredom. I started writing when I was fourteen, and had just finished a particularly long day in secondary school. Cold Blood is not my first book; my first was a story called "The diary of a werewolf", which was unintentionally a copy of the movie "An American werewolf in London".

2.Have you *always* wanted to be a writer?

No, I have not always wanted to be a writer. I just decided one day to share some of my writing, because I wanted to see what some people I respect would think. I began writing more when I found out they liked it until one day, during lockdown because of the COVID-19 pandemic, I decided to try and publish. Inspired by the author Myria Candies.

3.Pantser or Planner?

I am a pantser, I tried at one point to plan a story; but I got stuck on the details of world-building, as it was a fantasy story with a world I wanted to be fully my own. When I realised that would be too much, I decided I would start writing and go wherever that took. I often joke that this means I am just as surprised by my plot twists as the reader will be.

4. Where do your characters come from? Are they based on people you know?

I try to avoid basing my characters on people I know, to make sure it's not too personal. I do this for two reasons. The first is because it means that I can write about the characters doing awful things, and having awful things happen to them, guilt-free. I don't want to say "I based a character on you, and they have all their limbs painfully removed!" The second is because it ensures that I can guess how likely the audience is to like a character based not on the person they are, but on the character themselves.

5.When do you write?

Wherever I can. The two biggest factors that prevent me from writing are the fact that I am university student— which means I have to spend hours a day away from my computer at university—, and the fact that I didnt alway have a computer to write on as the one I wrote most of Cold Blood on was over forty miles away for most of my time in university,

6. How did you come up with your book title?

Cup of Sleep

The idea behind the title was a metaphor, cup of sleep meaning a cup of coffee as the setting of the story is one that uses coffee in place of sleep to an unhealthy degree. This was the title of the story throughout the whole thing unlike Cold Blood which had a different title when it first began.

7. How did you come up with the idea for Cup of Sleep?
There were two main sources of inspiration for Cup of Sleep was foremost my dislike of the book 1984 by George Orwell as I found it to be a boring book, and secondly by how many people had told me they couldn't survive without coffee. I wanted to take their obvious exaggeration and make it literal.

8.What's the most difficult part of writing for you?
Responding to feedback, specifically in cases where the feedback from some readers contradicts the one given by others. I soon learned it was about which bit of feedback you choose to go with, because at the end of the day, the feedback is just their opinion.

9. How do you research your book if at all?

I did a small amount of research for the story, mostly about the side effects of sleep deprivation but didn't stick too close to it given the sci-fi dystopian nature of the story.

10.Can you share something from your book that isn't a blurb?

There was a bigger focus on diversity of characters in this story than in any of my other stories including diversity of race, gender and sex as the people I spend time talking too has become more diverse.

11.We will get our first criticism or bad review at some point. How do you handle literary criticism or poor reviews?

My bad habit when I get negative feedback is that I try to fix all of it, which is difficult; both because, as previously mentioned, it can be contradictory, and because I can be annoying for the readers, as it requires me to constantly ask for clarification.

12.What is the most surprising thing you've discovered as an author?

The most annoying part of writing is everything that surrounds writing: things like designing covers, editing, formatting and promotion. The easiest part of writing is the actual writing. Luckily, in the case of Cold Blood, I had help from the lovely Myria Candies, so these things weren't as big of a problem as they could have been. When I tried to, for example, make my own cover I found that I was not artistic at all. However I didn't have the same amount of help with Cup of Sleep so I need to do significantly more of the work myself.

13. Who is your favourite, out of the characters you have written?

I don't have a favourite character but out of everyone who has read it so far has said that their favourite character is Danni, the long suffering mother and recent widow.

14. What do you hope your readers take away from your book?

The main theme is the idea that one's health should not be compromised in the name of productivity which includes getting a good night of sleep no matter what work you might have to do as a lack of sleep can worsen both your health and quality of work.

Cup of Sleep

210210Andrew James King

Acknowledgment

There are many people I would like to thank for helping me with the creation of this story starting with the writers and readers of amino who read my early drafts and gave me feedback and encouragement when I started having doubts.

I would also like to thank the people who read and reviewed my last book. The fact that people were willing to spend money to read something I had written spoke volumes.

I'd like to thank Farris of wholesomefilmtalk for the daily reminder to give myself permission to make something bad, not because I did make something bad but because it helped me stop worrying about it being bad and just write.

I would like to thank my beta readers, the people who read the earlier drafts and told me honestly what they thought of the story.

The last person I would like to thank is you, the reader. I am an unknown writer, so just the fact that you were willing to give my book a chance is big. For that, I thank you.

211211Andrew James King

Printed in Great Britain
by Amazon